"I thought journalists were supposed to keep their distance."

Gil reached out to tuck a strand of hair behind Jillian's ear. "Maybe I don't want to keep my distance."

Jillian swallowed. "I'm talking about work."

"I'm not," he said softly.

He was too close, and there wasn't enough air. "Why me?" she asked.

"Oh, maybe because you're gorgeous." He traced his fingertip down her nose. "Smart." The finger continued along the groove of her upper lip. "Funny." He traced the outline of her lips, leaning closer. "Caring." He curved his fingers around the back of her neck, drawing her closer. "And incredibly sexy."

Heat and tension began to coil inside her.

"I can't stop thinking about you," Gil murmured. "I dream about you at night. I wake up wanting you."

Helplessly she stared at him, her lips parting.

And then his mouth was on hers....

Dear Reader,

When I was little, I used to love dressing up in my mother's clothes, putting on her scarves and high heels and parading around. This month, I'm stepping into another pair of big shoes with *Always a Bridesmaid.* I was thrilled when the editors invited me to write the final chapter for LOGAN'S LEGACY REVISITED—thrilled to be included with a group of such talented authors and thrilled to tell the story of Jillian, Gil and the rest of the Logan clan. To prepare, I spent two weeks in Portland with my older sister, who selflessly spent time taking me to brewpubs, restaurants, the Chinese Garden and a host of other sights in the area.

Drop me a line at Kristin@kristinhardy.com and let me know what you think. Stop by www.kristinhardy.com for news, recipes and contests, or to sign up for my newsletter, which includes information about my new releases.

Enjoy!

Kristin Hardy

ALWAYS A BRIDESMAID

KRISTIN HARDY

SPECIAL EDITION®

Published by Silhouette Books

America's Publisher of Contemporary Romance

Special thanks and acknowledgment are given
to Kristin Hardy for her contribution to the
LOGAN'S LEGACY REVISITED miniseries.

 SILHOUETTE BOOKS

ISBN-13: 978-0-373-28080-3
ISBN-10:   0-373-28080-7

ALWAYS A BRIDESMAID

Visit Silhouette Books at www.eHarlequin.com

Printed in U.S.A.

KRISTIN HARDY

Book-crazy her whole life, Kristin Hardy started her first novel, about a boy and his horse, at 12. The key word is "started." In the early 1980s, she set her cap at becoming a romance writer, but it wasn't until 2001 that she actually finished a book. The result, *My Sexiest Mistake,* sold to Harlequin Books in a week, made the Waldenbooks bestseller list, won a National Readers' Choice Award and debuted as a movie on the Oxygen Network. Kristin lives in New Hampshire with her husband, a nationally recognized consultant on all things guy.

ACKNOWLEDGMENTS

Thanks go to
Jessica Felts of On Demand Limousine
Ed Scheiner of the Las Vegas Wedding Chapel
and especially to Barbara Drotos, LICSW
for helping bring this story to life

To Karen,
fifteen two, fifteen four
And to Stephen,
for always paying his departure fees promptly

Chapter One

"I've always loved babies." Shelly Dolan's voice shook. Next to her on the overstuffed sage-green sofa, her husband, Doug, reached out to put his arm around her shoulders. "I loved playing with them, holding them, making them laugh. They were just a delight. But now, every time I see a stroller, every time I see a pregnant woman, it feels like something's breaking inside of me." Her breath began to hitch "All I can do is cry. And Doug—"

Jillian Logan, social worker at the Children's Connection fertility and adoption clinic, stirred in her deep, soft chair. "What about Doug?" she asked.

"His shop is right down the street from a preschool. And his car's been on the fritz this week so I've been having to take him to work. And to drive by every day and see— And see— And see—" Her voice caught and she buried her face in Doug's shoulder for a moment.

It squeezed Jillian's heart. "It must be hard," she said softly.

"I never guessed," Shelly whispered. "And Doug's always so strong, I worry that he's holding it all in."

"What's it like for you, going through this?" Jillian asked Doug.

Next to his neat, dark wife, he looked burly and ill at ease. He'd come straight from work and still wore his stained welder's clothing. And he was there, clearly, only because of Shelly.

"Hell, Doc, how do you think your husband—" he glanced at her ringless fingers "—or boyfriend or whoever would feel? How would you feel?" he challenged.

"We're not here to talk about me, Doug." Jillian's voice was gentle.

Over the seven months since the Dolans had been coming to the Children's Connection in hopes of having a child, Jillian had watched their expressions morph from irrepressible hope to disappointment to a kind of grim determination. Now a faint air of strain hung about them.

But they were still together, still getting one another through.

"You want to know how I feel?" Doug asked now. "Worried. About Shelly, I mean. I don't think we need to waste our time here talking about me."

"You're going through it, too. You're both involved."

His jaw tightened. "I'm okay."

"You spent the entire week going on about Roy's son," Shelly reminded him.

"What about Roy's son?" Jillian asked.

Doug made a noise of frustration. "My boss's kid. The little punk knocked up his girlfriend. Sixteen. Too stupid to wear a condom, the idiot."

"Why does it make you so angry?"

"They're too young to have a kid. Hell, they're kids themselves. Either they keep it and really mess up their lives or she gives it up, or she gets rid of it. Idiot. All because he couldn't keep it in his pants. And it's such a freaking crock," he said with sudden savagery.

"What is?"

"He's sixteen and he can get his girlfriend pregnant. I'm thirty-five and we want a kid so much and I damned well can't give my wife a baby." Doug leaned forward and put his head in his hands.

Jillian waited in the humming silence. This was the moment she'd been working toward for months, a chance to finally get Doug to open up. And yes, the session was supposed to be ending but there was no way she was going to punch the clock on this one. "It's okay to feel angry or guilty or out of control, Doug. The feelings are real. You're allowed."

He was silent for another moment, then he let out a breath. "I'm fine," he said quietly, straightening. "We'll get through it." He glanced at his watch. "Anyway, our time's up, isn't it, Doc?"

"I don't know, is it?"

He nodded slowly, his eyes on her. "Yeah. I think so."

Reluctantly, Jillian rose to move to her desk. "Think about what we've talked about here today. You're getting close to something, Doug, and I don't think we should just let it go. Let's talk about it more next week."

"Yeah, sure, whatever." He shepherded Shelly hastily out of the office.

And Jillian watched them go out together.

Together. That was the key. However difficult the emotional challenges, the two of them were still a team. They walked down the hall, Doug's arm around Shelly's shoulders. How would it feel to have that comfort? Jillian wondered, that sense that whatever you faced, you did it as a part of a whole?

How do you think your husband or boyfriend or whoever would feel?

She wouldn't know, because Jillian didn't have one. She never had.

She thought of her missing stepbrother Robbie, manager of the day care center at the Children's Connection, part of her adoptive family. The stepbrother she hadn't seen in over a month, ever since he'd walked out on his wife, the clinic, his family, driven away by the scandalous past he couldn't escape. Why hadn't Robbie been able to trust that they would be there for him?

Maybe because, like Jillian, he bore scars from the childhood years spent outside the Logan nest. Childhood trauma could haunt you, Jillian knew. Like the dark times she and her twin brother, David, had suffered before Terrence and Leslie Logan had adopted them at age six.

There was a tap at the door and Jillian glanced up to see Lois Carella, the senior social worker at the clinic, peering in. "Do you have a minute to talk about the Podracki birth-parent letter?"

Jillian checked her watch. "I'm sorry, it'll have to wait until Monday. I'm supposed to be at a wedding rehearsal in a half hour."

"Another one? You're in more weddings than anyone I know."

Didn't she know it. It was the curse of the therapist. No one knew how to give better friendship. Jillian was unparalleled at being a friend.

It was just the part about accepting friendship in return that she wasn't so good at.

"Who is it this time?" Lois asked.

"Lisa Sanders. She's marrying some tycoon from Texas."

Lois laughed. "The Texas tycoon. Sounds like the title of a romance novel."

"A bit, I suppose. Except for the part where the *Gazette* dragged Lisa's name in the mud." The *Portland Gazette,* the same newspaper that had dredged up Robbie's own history with a babynapping ring, the newspaper that had driven him away.

"I seem to remember they corrected things, though, didn't they?"

"I suppose." A spurious lawsuit from the father of the child Lisa had borne and adopted out as an unwed, homeless teen had turned into a biased, inflammatory front-page story. Eventually, the *Gazette* had gotten to the truth of the matter and cleared Lisa's name. Eventually. "Too bad they didn't do the same with Robbie."

"Don't blame the *Gazette.* It's the tabloids and the television shows that have been hounding him."

"It doesn't matter. He's gone." And once again, Jillian's family was torn apart. Once again, her adoptive parents were racked over Robbie, their son kidnapped as a child, rediscovered as an adult struggling to find the right path. Jillian was a licensed clinical social worker, for God's sake, she had years of counseling experience. And yet she hadn't been able to help him. She couldn't heal where it counted.

"Don't do that to yourself," Lois said quietly.

Jillian straightened her shoulders. "Do what?"

"You demand too much of yourself, Jillian. You always have." Lois's eyes softened. "He's going to be okay, you'll see. It'll work out."

"I hope you're right."

"Of course I am," Lois said briskly. "I always am. Now get off to your wedding. And Jillian?"

"What?"

"Don't forget to catch the bouquet. I think it's your turn now."

The stained glass windows threw patches of glowing red and blue and green light over the polished wood of the pews. The very air of the church held a quiet serenity, an indefinable hush. Jillian should have felt uplifted. She should have felt joy for Lisa and Alan.

Instead, all she felt was lonely.

Which was ridiculous. Ninety-nine percent of the time—okay, at least fifty or sixty percent, she admitted—she was fine being alone. She preferred it, actually. She'd looked, but she'd never found her match. She'd grown happiest once she'd given up trying. She was one of those people who was best on her own, it was that simple. She'd had thirty-three years to get used to the idea.

So why was the thought of being single and watching one more happy couple pledge their lives to one another breaking her heart?

Not that she wasn't happy for her friends. She was, she could say without doubt. But there was something now that struck her to her very core, something about knowing she'd never be the one walking down the aisle toward a groom who stood bright-eyed in expectation, that at the reception to come she'd have no date, no boyfriend, no husband, no one who cared for her above all. No matter. She'd smile and hold her head high. And she'd joke and dance the choreographed dances, walk with her fingertips on the arm of her usher, touching a man, something she did so seldom—aside from her brothers—that it belonged in the headlines.

And go home feeling more desperately lonely than at any other time in her life. Maybe it was Robbie being gone. Maybe it was the turmoil her family was in. Maybe it was just her.

With a sigh, Jillian glanced over to where Lisa Sanders, the bride-to-be, paced nervously.

"I wish he would just get here," Lisa said,

raking her fingers through her blond hair. "We only have the church for another ten minutes. Alan," she appealed to her fiancé, "can't you please call him?"

"Who?" Jillian asked.

"We're missing an usher. Alan's friend, Gil."

Tall and sandy and Texan, Alan exuded calm control. "I talked with him this afternoon and he said he was going to be here."

"Maybe something's come up. Anyway, our dinner reservation is half an hour after we get done here, so we've got to stay on schedule."

"Hey," Jillian said softly as Lisa's pacing route brought her near, "it's going to be okay." Normally, Lisa was organized to within an inch of her life. Normally, she was as cool as could be. There was something about weddings, though, that broke the nerves of the calmest person. And Lisa was only twenty-one, Jillian reminded herself.

"I know, I know, I'm worrying about nothing," Lisa said too quickly. "It's just all the details that are driving me crazy. I mean, I know five o'clock was a bad time for the rehearsal but it was the only one they had. We put this together so quickly. And we've got to get all the centerpieces over to the reception hall and I need to tie up the favors and I still have to do the holder for the place cards. And I hung my dress from my ceiling light fixture so it wouldn't wrinkle and I just know it's fallen down by now and it's in a pile all over the floor and—"

"And all that matters is the 'I do' part," Alan drawled, coming up from behind to slide an arm around her waist. "Forget about the centerpieces. Forget about the place cards. Hell, we can skip it all, if you want. My corporate jet could have us in Vegas in three hours. Get married tonight and come back tomorrow for the party."

Lisa laughed and turned to kiss him. "You have no idea how tempting that sounds. But everyone's here and the arrangements are already made. We'll get through it. You're sweet, though." She kissed him again.

"And you're beautiful," he replied. "We make a good pair."

Together, Jillian thought, just like Doug and Shelly. "Can't we rehearse without Alan's friend?" she suggested to Lisa as Alan walked away, flipping open his cell phone. "Let's run through it with the people who are here. The Invisible Man can figure things out tomorrow."

"I suppose. It's just that he's supposed to be first usher, right next to Neal." Neal Barrett, Alan's brother and best man.

"I'd say the Invisible Man just got demoted for tardiness," Jillian told her. "You show up more than twenty—" she consulted her watch "—twenty-five minutes late, you take your chances."

"I agree," said Carrie Summers, walking up from behind. Carrie had that brisk, take-charge air that mothers seemed to acquire. Of course, it made sense. Carrie was practically like a second mother to Lisa, ever since they'd met when Carrie and her husband, Brian, were adopting Lisa's son, Timothy. Somehow birth mother and adoptive parents had become friends, then family. And Lisa, who'd lost both parents to an auto accident when she'd been young, had a home again.

"Let's reshuffle things," Carrie said now. "Besides," she added sotto voce, "if we leave everyone in the order you've got them, we'll have Jillian towering over her escort." She nodded at the short, stocky guy standing across the way. "A switch would be better, assuming Alan's friend is tall."

Tall enough for a five-nine woman wearing heels, to be exact. Yet another reason Jillian had never quite fit in. "Well, if he's not here, I can't very well be taller than him, now can I?" she asked.

"Oh, Gil's taller than you," Lisa said distractedly, watching her fiancé. "I think he's even taller than Alan."

"Then it's settled." Carrie briskly shooed the ushers toward the altar. "We'll match him up with Jillian."

"It's a straight shot down the aisle," Jillian said drily. "I'm pretty sure I can find my way on my own if I have to. And if not, I'll just hitch a ride with Christina's usher."

"I'll arm wrestle you for him," Christina, Alan's college-aged daughter offered, laughter in her blue eyes.

The usher in question, standing nearby, frowned. "If I was a chick, you'd be screaming sexism," he complained.

"But you're not a chick, so you should be flattered," Christina said, giving him a saucy look from under her lashes.

"You take him, Christina," Jillian said, getting into position at the end of the line of bridesmaids. "I'll make it on my own."

Just as she always had.

Gil Reynolds typed furiously, his fingers clattering swift and sure on the keyboard, and then leaned back to read what he'd written.

Snow & Taylor Construction, contractors for the billion-dollar downtown Portland streetcar line slated to begin construction this fall, may have won the project without a proper bid process, according to recent documents unearthed by the *Gazette*.

His favorite kind of story, blowing the lid off corruption in city government. He had his facts up front, a couple of source quotes. Just the way he liked it. Of course, it was still missing that certain something.

A comment from the guest of honor.

With a smile, Gil pushed his dark hair back off his forehead and reached out to dial the phone.

"Yeah?" a man's voice answered brusquely.

"Nash? Gil Reynolds from the *Gazette*. We're running a story on possible fraud in the contracting of the streetcar project. According to the transcripts I saw, Snow & Taylor managed to get the project without competitive bidding."

Charlie Nash, city councillor. Better than a few, worse than most. There was a pause while Nash took it in. "Reynolds? What the hell are you doing calling me? I thought you were an editor now. You get busted back down?"

"Filling in for one of my reporters who's on compassionate leave."

"You don't have a compassionate bone in your body," the city councillor growled.

Gil's teeth gleamed. "Now, come on, Charlie, aren't we friends? I figured this story was a good chance for us to catch up. Snow & Taylor dumped a lot of money into your campaign, didn't they?"

"You're a menace."

Gil leaned back in his chair. "Maybe you should

get that put on a plaque. I could hang it on the wall next to my Pulitzer."

"You run that story, I'll sue."

"I'm just running the facts. What makes you think there'll be anything to sue about? That sounds like a guilty conscience talking. Come on, you'll feel better if you confess to Uncle Gil."

"In a pig's eye. Why don't you go after O'Donnell?"

"O'Donnell wasn't heading the appropriations committee when the contract got let. You were, and your buddies got the job without even trying. Seems to me like the public ought to know. I wanted to be fair and give you a chance to air your side, though. You could set the record straight. Or should I just call for an audit? You got some state and federal bucks for the project, didn't you?"

"You piranha."

Gil grinned. "Can I quote you on that, Nash?"

"You can quote me on this." When the line clicked, Gil chuckled. Merrily, he tapped away, listening to the hubbub of the newsroom outside his office door. In these, the waning hours before deadline, the room was gripped with a feverish purpose, everyone working as quickly as they could to get the paper together and out the door. Not the least of which was him, given that he'd been trying to fill in for two people ever since Mark's father had had his fatal heart attack.

"I need that streetcar story." Ron Bates, his copy editor, stood at the door impatiently. "And the Willamette pollution story and the Logan piece."

"The streetcar story should be in your in-box."

"What about the other two?"

"Soon," Gil promised.

"How soon?"

"Gee, let me get my magic wand out and see. Look, I'm going to need at least fifteen minutes to go through them."

Ron glowered. "You make me miss deadline and the press manager will be coming after me. Which means I'll be coming after you."

"Anyone ever tell you that you're beautiful when you're angry, Ron?"

"Kiss my ass," his copy editor said, and turned away.

Grinning, Gil picked up the ringing phone. "Reynolds."

"Gil, this is Alan. Alan Barrett? You know, your college buddy who's getting married tomorrow? The guy whose rehearsal started half an hour ago? That guy?"

Gil snapped his head around to stare at the clock, which had somehow vaulted forward an hour and a half since he'd last checked it. He uttered a heartfelt curse.

"That's one way of putting it."

"Hell, Alan, I'm sorry. One of my reporters just lost his dad and I'm filling in while he's gone. I lost track of time. Deadlines are biting my ass today." Gil sent off the first of the articles.

"Yeah, well, I've got a deadline here, too. And a fiancée who's working on an ulcer. You thinking about gracing us with your presence any time this year?"

"I'll be there in—" he calculated quickly "—twenty minutes. Twenty five."

Now it was Alan's turn to curse. "Forget about the church. We'd be leaving by the time you got here."

"I'm really sorry, Alan."

"I know. Look, come to the dinner, at least, so you get a chance to meet everyone. It's at the Odeon. You know, the new McMillan's place?"

"Wouldn't miss it for the world."

Chapter Two

One thing Jillian could say for Alan, he knew how to throw a rehearsal dinner. Forget about a discreet restaurant back room. Instead, he'd taken the upper balcony of the Odeon Tango Theater, the newest in the McMillan brothers' chain of brewpub hotels. The old Thirties movie palace had been completely renovated, from the trompe l'oeil and molded-plaster ceiling to the gold-leafed moldings to the deep burgundy curtains that covered the stage.

The tables on the balcony were arranged to accommodate the wedding party and the various out-of-town relatives and friends of Alan's who'd been invited. At the gleaming walnut bar against the wall, the bartender pulled pints of the McMillan's award-winning beers. On the tables, bottles of champagne chilled in ice buckets, readily at hand for the rash of toasts that were already taking place.

That was fine with Jillian. In her current mood, it was easy to substitute sipping champagne for conversation. Not that it was necessarily a smart move, especially since drinking wasn't normally her thing. Champagne, even with its effervescent bubbles, wouldn't banish the loneliness. Champagne wouldn't banish the memory of the pang she'd felt when she'd walked back up the aisle all alone, toward the laughing crowd of paired-up bridesmaids and ushers. Sure, it was just the wedding rehearsal, but in a way it was a reflection of her life. She wasn't a part of the laughing crowd, she wasn't a part of a pair.

She never had been.

When, she wondered with a thread of desperation, would it change?

When you make it change.

She knew the textbook explanation for why she kept people at arm's length—raised in squalor, abandoned at four with her twin brother, David, by their mother, neglected by their stroke-ridden grandmother, raised to feel unimportant, unloved, unwanted.

Unworthy.

She knew it was irrational. And as a therapist, she knew how difficult it was to root out feelings grown from the seeds of childhood trauma, however irrational the adult knew them to be.

As a therapist, she also knew that sometimes you had to go out of your comfort zone first to make yourself change. That had been Lois's point; Lois, who had known Jillian since the Logans had adopted her. At a certain point you needed to move on with your life. Drinking champagne wouldn't change the fact that she was alone. Doing something different would. If being alone hurt, then she needed to open the gates that she kept locked shut against the world.

I'm afraid.

It was ridiculous, of course, she thought, watching Carrie Summers laugh with her husband, Brian, watching Lisa and Alan as they leaned in for a kiss. What was there to fear? They were glowing with happiness, with the sheer wonder of being parts of a whole.

And suddenly, desperately, Jillian wanted to know what that feeling was like.

An intelligent woman would do something about it. That was what the therapist side of her would suggest if she were in a session with herself. Make a plan and execute it. Go on a blind date. Ask someone she knew to fix her up. Hell, say hello to a guy once in a while.

Of course, if she were in a session with herself, it might be time to consider medication for multiple personality disorder, she thought. And she surprised herself with a hiccup.

A couple of places down from Jillian's spot at the end of the table, Lisa turned, eyes wide. "Was that a hiccup I just heard?"

"It's nothing," Jillian told her, surprised that she had to work just a bit to make the words come out clearly.

Down on the stage, the curtains parted to reveal a stunningly beautiful brunette partnered with a man dressed in a black shirt and trousers. They stood, pressed against one another and, slowly, they began to dance.

She never touched anyone, Jillian thought. Oh, she hugged her mother and her sister, Bridget, now and again, or maybe a girlfriend. That was about it. Her world was so small: don't touch, don't look too hard at anyone, don't make eye contact for too long in case it's too much. Because without the freedom of having that one person into whose eyes she could gaze, that one person she could hold on to without worrying, all contact with other people seemed perilously complex. How much was too much? How much would inadvertently cross the line because she no longer knew where that line was?

When she was at work, in sessions, she felt confident. Anywhere else, forget it.

The dancers whirled in the tango, twining around one another in the choreographed seduction of the dance. Even up in the balcony, Jillian could feel the heat, the sexuality. What must it be like to want and be wanted? She was thirty-three and she'd never been intimate with a man. Kisses, yes. She'd even felt a man's hands touch her body, if you could call the clumsy college boy she'd fooled around with one night a man. She'd read about sex, she'd even counseled patients, but she knew nothing about it from personal experience.

She knew nothing about relationships, at all.

It wasn't right, Jillian thought suddenly, watching the dancers. It wasn't right that she didn't know, it wasn't right that she hadn't even tried to change things. She was a social worker, a skilled therapist. She should do better.

Why not? she thought, feeling suddenly bold, and tossed off the rest of her champagne. Why not try going after what she wanted?

It's your turn now.

"Hot, huh?"

Jillian turned to see Lisa's maid of honor, Ariel, looking as mischievous as Peter Pan with her spiky brunette pixie cut and her sparkling eyes.

"They're pretty amazing," Jillian said. The flow of dancers' bodies, their silky-looking touches gave her a little flicker of excitement just watching. "I'd love to learn."

"Oh, me, too. I think they give lessons after the show. We ought to come sometime when we can try it out."

"What if I don't have a partner?"

Ariel laughed. "Like that's a problem? Just smile at a guy and grab him by the arm."

Jillian looked at Ariel in admiration. Was it really that simple for her? It seemed extraordinary. There was no way Jillian could ever work up that much nerve, not immediately. Smiling, maybe. She could start with smiling. Whereupon she'd probably be standing around forever. "They should set it up like one of those dime-a-dance places from World War II. That way you wouldn't have to worry."

"Dime a dance? Try a five spot, at least." Ariel's eyes brightened. "Ooh, just imagine if it was like one of those vending machines where you use the lever thing to pick out exactly who you want. Just put your money in the slot and—"

"Darn it!" Jillian slapped her forehead.

"What?"

"I totally forgot. I've got to go feed my meter. I didn't have any change when I parked," she explained, digging in her purse for a dollar. "I meant to go right back out."

"Drinking champagne will do that to you. Anyway, why are you worried? This late, no one cares."

"It's only six-thirty." Jillian rose. "And trust me, if anyone's going to get a parking ticket at six fifty-nine, it'll be me."

Downstairs, she walked out the front door and through the old-fashioned half-moon movie-house entryway with its central ticket booth. On the street, the late afternoon was bleeding into June dusk as the sun dipped toward the horizon. The clouds of the morning had burned away. The air felt soft and welcoming.

She'd taken off her jacket inside and the breeze fluttered through the claret silk tank she wore beneath. It felt good to move. It would have felt good to dance, if she'd only known how. She felt a sudden, restless urge for something new.

Her meter, she could see from a few cars away, was firmly over into redline territory. But she was less interested in that than the guy a bit beyond, walking down the sidewalk toward her. Tall, dark, moving with an easy assurance, he wore a jacket and tie and sunglasses. The breeze blew his dark hair onto his forehead; he raised an impatient hand to rake it back.

This was it, Jillian thought. She wanted to make a change? Now was her chance. Just a small change. All she had to do was glance at him and smile. Simple enough. Something millions of women did every day. Once she got used to that behavior, she'd move on. For now, just a smile. That wasn't much, was it?

So why was her heart hammering?

Jillian stood at her meter, fumbling with her coins. He was closer now. Almost time. It wasn't as if it was a military operation, she thought impatiently. She just needed to look at him and do it, as if it was natural. Natural.

Hah.

She glanced up, preparing to smile. And froze.

Handsome was the wrong word. Handsome was too tepid, a description for men with perfect Ken-doll looks. His was a face that was more about purpose and intent, pure force of personality. Strong bones, straight nose, a chin that looked as though it knew how to take a punch. His eyes were hidden by his sunglasses. His mouth was straight and wide and far too intriguing.

And then he smiled and the coins slipped through her suddenly nerveless fingers.

With a noise of frustration, Jillian bent to grab for them, trying fruitlessly to capture the rolling disks before they went over the curb and through the grate beyond.

"Need some help?"

Adrenaline vaulted through her system. He'd stopped. The guy had stopped and now he was bent down by her meter, trying to retrieve the coins. "I think they're all on their way to the Columbia River by now," she said.

"Slippery devils," he said, pushing up his glasses and grinning.

She could hear her pulse thudding in her ears. His eyes were black, she saw, his dark brows quirked now with just a hint of humor.

He handed her a quarter. "There's one, anyway."

Her hand was shaking as she took the coin from him. Okay, this was more than she'd planned. It was supposed to be a smile and glance, not a whole discussion. She wasn't sure she was up for a full discussion, especially after all the champagne.

She rose.

"What about your other quarter?" He nodded at the meter as he stood. "One won't take you through the witching hour."

"I guess I'll just have to take my chances."

"Feeling lucky, huh?" He grinned, and she felt

something in her stomach flip. Lethal smile, absolutely lethal. And without warning she found herself staring at his upper lip and wondering just what it would be like to kiss him.

Lucky? "I guess I am," she said. It was the champagne, she told herself. Starting up her own personal perestroika campaign was one thing, picking up men on the street was another.

But he was already rummaging in his pocket to pull out a handful of coins.

"You can't pay my meter," she objected.

"Sure I can," he said as he picked through the change for a quarter and put it in. "It's good karma. After a day like I've had, I could use it."

"Uh-oh," she said. "That doesn't sound good."

"Uh-oh, is right. If you see a lynch mob coming out of the Odeon, they'll be looking for me."

"Is that where you're going?" she asked, falling in step beside him as they walked the dozen yards to where the light from the theater's marquee spilled over the sidewalk.

"Yep. How about you?"

She nodded.

"I'd offer to buy you a drink but I'm here for a party. Actually, I'm late for a party," he corrected. "Really late."

"That's okay, I'm here with—" She broke off and gave him a suspicious stare. "What kind of a party?"

"Me?" He held the door for her. "A rehearsal dinner, for a wedding. Why?"

She walked through, the little buzz of excitement fading. "Your name wouldn't happen to be Gil, would it?"

"Guilty as charged. And you are?"

"Jillian Logan, the bridesmaid you left at the altar. Nice of you to finally join us."

Gil's lips twitched as he followed her into the lobby. "Left you at the altar, huh? Did I have a brain fade? Were we getting married?"

"I'm not likely to marry the kind of guy who'd show up—" she checked her watch "—over an hour late to his best friend's wedding rehearsal."

"I guess it's a good thing I never proposed, then. It was touch-and-go out there."

She gave him a look from under her brows. "You know, you had the bride wearing a groove in the carpet pacing over you? Lisa's got enough going on right now without one more thing to stress about."

His amusement dipped a bit. "I know, trust me."

She folded her arms, a bit like a teacher scolding a wayward student. "Not to mention the fact that we were all standing around waiting."

"Not to mention," he agreed. And she was ticked. Protective of Lisa and just a little ticked about waiting around. Or maybe the altar thing. He wasn't sure just why he found that appealing. Maybe it was because he found *her* appealing. Her mouth for a start, full and tempting, the lower lip just a bit sulky now. It had been the first thing he'd noticed when he first saw her. When she'd smiled at him by the meter, he'd felt the hit down deep.

And those eyes of hers, the color of good whiskey. They looked enormous and he didn't think it was just tricky makeup. They were turbulent now with challenge, enough to promise she'd give him a run for his money. And she had that thick, dark hair with the red undertones of good mahogany. The kind of hair a man could bury his hands in.

Her chin came up a bit as she noticed him staring. He didn't bother to fight the smile. She was tall for a woman, slender enough that at a glance a person would judge her fragile. It was an impression he was betting drove her nuts. She didn't look like the type who wanted to be taken care of. She looked like the type who liked being in control.

Funny, so was he.

"I guess I started off on the wrong foot with you here. Except for the quarter at the meter," he added. "I should get some points for that."

"It's going to take more than a quarter to make up for missing the wedding rehearsal," she told him.

"And leaving you at the altar. I could escort you up the stairs," he offered as they skirted the velvet rope that blocked off the balcony. "That's a start."

She glanced at his arm. "I can make it up the stairs on my own."

"I bet you can," he said, resisting the urge to linger a bit behind her and admire the view. "It would be more fun with me, though."

She rolled her eyes. "Are you always like this?"

"You're going to break down and laugh sooner or later. You may as well give in to the inevitable."

She turned to him at the top of the stairs. "And that is?"

He gazed down into those whiskey-gold eyes. "I'll let you know."

And suddenly, as she stared back at him, the joking slipped away and something else flashed in its place, a hard, deep pulse of wanting that momentarily banished everything else. Something hummed between them, like a subsonic vibration that he could neither hear nor see, but only feel.

And the flicker in her eyes told him she felt it, too.

"About time you showed," a voice drawled from behind him and Alan walked up.

Gil blinked and the moment was gone. He turned to the tall Texan. "Hey, sorry I'm late," he said as they shook.

"And here I thought you were a pretty sorry specimen already," Alan said. "Glad to see you finally found the place."

"You made it," Lisa said, stepping up alongside Alan.

"I did," Gil said. Instead of shaking her hand, he bowed down to kiss it. "I really apologize for missing the rehearsal. Major screwup. You've got a lot to worry about right now and the last thing you need is more grief from me."

"Hey, no putting the moves on my fiancée," Alan protested.

"Especially," Gil went on, ignoring Alan, "since you're going to have plenty of grief, already, with marrying this guy off."

Lisa laughed delightedly and pressed a kiss to Gil's cheek. "Oh, don't worry about it. Alan can tell you where you're supposed to stand tomorrow and I'm sure you can figure out the rest. Why don't you come meet everybody and have some champagne? Dinner's just starting."

Out of the corner of his eye, Gil noticed Jillian drift off to her seat.

Probably just as well, he thought. As an editor at the *Gazette,* the last thing he needed was to get anything going with Jillian Logan. He'd already been warned.

So he met the rest of the party, laughing, joking,

shaking hands. And did his best to forget that strange snap of connection at the top of the stairs.

"This is Ariel, Lisa's good friend," Alan said, bringing him to the last table.

"And best chick," Ariel added.

"Maid of honor," Alan translated. "And you already know Jillian, here."

"Informally," Gil said. He extended his hand. "Gil Reynolds, meter caddy."

"Jillian Logan, usher wrangler." She reached out.

Her hand was soft and cool in his. It felt fragile but he'd been right about the strength that underlaid it. He'd expected that.

He hadn't expected it to be trembling.

In surprise, his gaze shot to hers and he saw her eyes widen before she glanced away. She tugged her hand to free it from his. Some perverseness made him hold on a moment longer than necessary, though, until she looked at him.

And he saw the gold of her eyes had darkened to deep amber.

Then he released her to nod down at the empty place setting at her side, the last one left. "Well, how about that? Looks like this is my seat."

This wasn't how it was supposed to go, Jillian thought with a mixture of giddiness and alarm as she concentrated on taking slow breaths to try to quiet her system. It was supposed to have been a smile on the street, a quick experiment, a little change—emphasis on *little*. It wasn't supposed to turn into anything. It definitely wasn't supposed to last the entire evening. And it certainly wasn't supposed to make her world feel as though it had tilted on its axis.

Surreptitiously, she rubbed at her right hand where it was hidden in her lap.

Forget about the quick, impersonal eye contact she'd perfected to keep people at a distance. Gil Reynolds's gaze had drilled right through her, right into her. And now he was sitting just inches away and she was supposed to be able to hold a conversation as if nothing had happened?

Nothing had, she reminded herself. He'd only been playing games.

Gil picked up the beer that the waiter brought him with the salad course and grinned. "To the happy couple," he said to Jillian.

She tapped his glass with her champagne flute. "To the happy couple," she said coolly.

"Come on, I apologized. See? I'm not a complete creep."

"I never said you were."

"Does that mean I'm forgiven?"

Jillian eyed him over the top of her glass. "I don't know. Should you be?"

Gil broke out laughing. "You're a tough case," he said. "Lisa forgave me."

"That's because you went all Continental and started kissing her hand."

"I'd be happy to kiss yours, too," he offered, a gleam in his eyes.

"No fair using the same trick twice," she objected, moving her hand hastily away. "Think up something else. Come on, you're a smart guy."

He eyed her. "This isn't going to be one of those quest things where I've got to go bring back a hair from the beard of the Great Chan, is it? Or find the Golden Fleece?"

"How about cleaning the stables of all the Budweiser Clydesdales in a single day? Of course, then you'd mess up that nice suit."

"Come on, cut me some slack. I'm a working schlemiel. Why do you think I was late?"

"What do you do?"

His mouth curved. "Make trouble."

"Why am I not surprised?" Her voice was dry. "And where do you make trouble?"

His grin widened. "Anywhere I can. No throwing things," he added quickly, as she reached for the basket of bread.

"That wasn't my intention," she said with dignity. "Although, now that you mention it…"

"Okay, okay. Blazon Media," he said, relenting.

"What, like an advertising agency? You're not one of those account exec types, are you?"

"That's a harsh way to talk about the people who help you decide how to spend your exorbitant salary."

"Exorbitant?" She couldn't prevent the snort.

"Or not," he added. "What do you do?"

"I'm a social worker."

"Okay, maybe not so exorbitant." He raised a brow. "A social worker, huh? And here I thought you guys were all softies."

"Here I thought you advertising types all had hundred-dollar haircuts and a closet full of Armani," she countered.

"I'm dressed down for casual Friday," he said.

"I'd hate to see you when you really put on the Ritz."

"Just wait until tomorrow." He winked. "Then you'll see my really grubby clothes."

The bartender leaned against the wall in his white apron and watched as the last of the rehearsal party left their tables and headed down the carpeted stairs. They'd closed the place down, Jillian realized in surprise, as she reached the bottom and turned for the lobby. She'd blinked once or twice and the hours had slipped away.

It was a shock, to say the least. Parties weren't her thing. To be honest, she'd looked forward to the rehearsal dinner with about as much enthusiasm as she would have a root canal. Outside of Lisa and Alan, she'd known no one. Somehow, though, that hadn't mattered. Forget about the usual rehearsal-dinner work of making conversation with people she didn't know and had little in common with. She'd spent the entire evening laughing.

And every time she'd turned to Gil, he'd been watching her with that little glimmer in his eyes.

He was beside her now as they walked out into the night. She tightened her jacket against the cool breeze. "I guess it's not quite summer yet."

"Give it another month and it will be," he said. They turned down the sidewalk toward her car. "You going to be okay driving?"

"Sure. I stopped with the champagne a while ago." Stopped early enough that her feet should be firmly grounded. Why was it, then, that she still felt the little bubbles of effervescence, that she felt like skipping?

"Good. Wouldn't want you to oversleep and miss my grand entrance at the wedding. I'm planning to be two hours early."

"Spoken like a true responsible citizen," she said.

"Making you proud of me is my life."

"It must have been dull until we met tonight,

then," she said lightly, turning to him as they reached her car.

"It was," he agreed. "I much prefer this." And suddenly he was looking at her with a look she couldn't quite categorize: speculation, anticipation, some special concentration.

Nerves vaulted through her. "Well, I guess you'd better get home and get dressed if you're going to be two hours early for the wedding, shouldn't you?"

He nodded, never taking his eyes off her. "I suppose so."

"It was nice to meet you." She concentrated on digging out her keys. If she did that, then she wouldn't focus on that mouth and wonder what it would be like to kiss him.

"It's nice to see you."

"It's late," she said desperately.

"Then I guess you'd better get going, Cinderella." With a flourish, he brought her hand to his lips and kissed it. Heat flashed through her. "See you at the altar."

Chapter Three

The dressing room smelled of cologne and hair spray, of freesia and lily of the valley from the bridal bouquets. Silk and tulle rustled below the chatter and buzz of a half-dozen women getting primped simultaneously.

"Lisa Sanders, have I told you how much I love and admire you?" Ariel turned to allow Jillian to zip up the back of her bridesmaid dress.

Lisa glanced over from where she sat at the vanity in the bride's dressing area. "Any particular reason now?"

"These dresses. They're gorgeous."

"I'll say," Jillian chimed in fervently. She'd been

in more weddings than she could count on one hand and had the closet full of poufy floral dresses to prove it. Lisa had rejected those horrors in favor of slim, tea-length dresses the color of the periwinkles in their bouquets.

Jillian glanced in the mirror at her own dress, admiring the way the bias-cut silk draped. "They really are lovely."

"And wait until your boy gets a load of you in that," Ariel said.

Jillian frowned. "My boy?"

"Gil," Ariel clarified. "I mean, the two of you were flirting like mad last night. Very hot."

It was crazy to get butterflies in her stomach at the thought of him, Jillian told herself. But every time she remembered the feel of his lips brushing over her knuckles, her stomach lurched as if she was in an elevator that was dropping too fast. She'd tried to tell herself it hadn't been a big deal. Sure he'd paid attention to her, walked her to her car, kissed her hand, but who knew what that meant? It could just be one of those things people did at rehearsal dinners.

But apparently she wasn't the only one who had noticed.

Maybe, Jillian thought, just maybe it hadn't been her imagination. Maybe there really had been that little buzz there, that little something that felt like, oh…

Chemistry.

It happened, she knew. Couples met, clicked and wound up dating. It wasn't just in movies and books; she heard about it from her patients, her girlfriends, even her siblings. People got involved, they had relationships.

Why not her?

"If I were you," Ariel continued, "I'd be looking forward to the reception. What do you think, Lisa?"

"I don't know." Lisa was focused intently on trying to get her pearl necklace out of its case but her hands were shaking too much to do it. She cleared her throat. "He's not really your type, Jillian, is he?"

Her type? How did she even know what her type was? He wasn't a standard pretty boy but she liked that. She liked the humor that was never far away, the way he made her laugh. And she really, really liked that buzz that went through her whenever they made eye contact.

But who was she fooling? What she liked most, what she hadn't been able to stop thinking of once since it had happened was the way it had felt when he'd brought her hand to his lips. Anticipation fluttered through her.

"He seems nice enough," she allowed.

Ariel snorted. "Nice enough?"

"Is he seeing anyone?" Jillian asked.

Lisa fumbled and dropped the necklace.

"Uh-oh, looks like prewedding jitters to me," Ariel said. "Anyone got a shot of vodka?"

"She doesn't need a drink." Jillian came over to help. "She just needs us to stop going on about everything else."

"I should have listened to Alan and gone to Vegas," Lisa moaned. "Everything would have been better."

"It's going to be beautiful," Jillian soothed, fastening the necklace in place and putting a reassuring hand on Lisa's shoulder. "You'll see. You're going to walk out there and see Alan and everything will be perfect."

Carrie came back into the room. "All right, everyone, it's time. Lisa, honey, you ready?"

"I think so." Lisa rose, touching her hair nervously. "How do I look?"

"Gorgeous," Jillian said, leaning in to kiss her cheek. "Be happy," she whispered.

Lisa gave her a tremulous smile. "I already am."

Gil stood in the dressing area watching Alan tie his tie. "So what do you say, are you ready to do this?"

"Of course. Why shouldn't I be?"

"Just checking. After all, it's my job as groomsman to prop you up in the bar and feed you a few drinks to get your courage up."

Alan patted Gil's shoulder. "I think you were supposed to do all that at the bachelor party."

Gil snapped his fingers. "Bachelor party. Damn. I knew there was something I forgot to do."

"I'll let it go," Alan said.

Gil studied his friend. "You're going to be happy, Alan," he said. "The two of you have a good vibe."

"Yeah?" For a minute, Alan forgot about the tie and met Gil's gaze in the mirror. "I keep wondering if I'm out of my mind, marrying a woman seventeen years younger than me. But I don't know, when I'm with her, it just works."

"I don't think you're out of your mind. She's smart, ambitious, gorgeous. And more grown-up than her age." Gil picked a bit of lint off his sleeve. "What she sees in you, of course, God only knows. If I were you, I'd marry her quick before she comes to her senses."

"Thanks for the vote of confidence."

"Anytime," Gil said cheerfully. "It's a good match. She can introduce you to the Raconteurs and you can introduce her to Tony Bennett and shuffleboard."

"I'll shuffle your board if you don't watch it," Alan growled.

"Hey, no roughing up the ushers."

Alan put on his jacket and buttoned it up. "I'll let you off the hook this time, but only because I have to go get married."

"Lucky me," Gil said.

"No," Alan said, "Lucky me."

White satin. Ribbons and lace. The church echoed with the liquid tones of the harp. Freesia from the bouquets scented the air. And everywhere faces glowed with that luminous joy unique to weddings.

Jillian stood quietly at the back of the church with the other bridesmaids. Behind them, hidden in an alcove, Lisa shifted nervously. Then the music started and Alan led the ushers out into place at the front of the church. There was a rustling as everybody turned to the back.

At Carrie's nod, Jillian began the measured walk down the aisle, the same one she'd made so many times before. Before her lay the pews, the ends adorned with bouquets and ribbons. Beyond that, she saw the organ, the altar, Alan and his ushers.

And Gil.

He wore a tuxedo, no different than the men beside him. But, oh, it looked different. Maybe it was his long, lean build, those shoulders, that way he had of standing as though he was totally at ease and at the same time ready for anything. His skin appeared very tanned, almost swarthy against the snowy-white of his shirt.

And he was staring right at her.

A whole squadron of butterflies took off to flutter madly about her stomach. He had that gleam in his eyes, that look that promised something special, she could see it from there. Quickly, she trained her gaze before her, on the altar. Having a bridesmaid going down the aisle staring at one of the ushers didn't exactly give a dignified look to the procession.

Focusing on the front of the church didn't help.

The fact that she kept her eyes turned from Gil was irrelevant—she was aware of him with every fiber of her being. She saw the white gleam of his smile, knew when he shifted a bit and clasped his hands together before him. Just taking each step took all her concentration, which was silly. It was only a look from across a room.

So why did it feel almost like a physical touch, one that strengthened with each inch she moved toward him?

The walk seemed endless, and yet Jillian was surprised to suddenly find herself at the end of the aisle. She took her place with relief and a sneaky little whiff of disappointment, as though a beam of sunlight had gone away. She was there for the wedding, she reminded herself, not a flirtation. Turning back to the aisle, she held her bouquet before her.

One by one, the other bridesmaids walked toward her and stepped into line. Including Ariel.

Who gave her a broad wink.

Jillian found herself stifling a giggle. Ariel just glided calmly and serenely into place. Only someone who was looking for it would have known that she was trying hard not to laugh, too.

And then the music swelled and there was a shuffle of feet as everyone stood for the bride.

She was, quite simply, lovely. As Lisa had chosen stylish simplicity for the bridesmaids' dresses, so she'd gone with simple elegance in her own attire: an ivory satin sheath, a garland of freesia and periwinkle for her hair. She was shaking visibly when she drew nearer, Jillian saw, her face pale, eyes huge. Then she reached the head of the aisle, and Brian Summers passed her hand to Alan.

And the moment their hands joined, the shakes were gone. Alan bent his head to kiss Lisa's fingers. Her smile bloomed, brilliant and beautiful as a sunrise.

Jillian found herself blinking back the sudden sting of tears.

Love. Honor. Cherish. Till death do us part. The

words flowed, the phrases that had always been a part of the lexicon of love, but suddenly they were real. She'd never believed in auras and all that mumbo jumbo, but when Alan and Lisa looked into each other's eyes, Jillian swore she could almost see their love for each other like a glowing nimbus that enveloped them both. It was real, this feeling, it existed. Blinking, she glanced beyond them.

Only to find her gaze pinned to Gil's.

His eyes were hot and dark and unwavering. And suddenly it was as if all the oxygen had been sucked out of the room. She couldn't breathe. She felt light-headed, suddenly dizzy as though the floor had tilted and his gaze were the only thing holding her in place. Everything around her receded. There was only Gil, looking at her and through her and into her.

The sound of applause broke the spell. Alan and Lisa were kissing, Jillian realized. The ceremony was finished and they were turning to march back up the aisle, hand in hand.

She glanced back to Gil to see his lips quirk in amusement. The recessional had begun, the bridesmaids and ushers walking forward to pair up, two by two, first Neal and Ariel, then the next pair and the next.

And then Gil was standing before her, offering his arm.

"Let the record show that here you are at the altar and here I am, right on time and ready to escort," he said.

Jillian laughed and the tension broke. "I appreciate that. I was worried about getting lost."

"And me, with no GPS."

She laid her hand on his sleeve. "I have faith in your sense of direction."

"Outstanding wedding," he said as they began to walk back up the aisle.

"It was." Particularly this part, with his arm strong and steady under her fingers, their steps falling in sync.

"Outstanding bridesmaids, too," Gil added. "Especially the first one that came down the aisle. The color of that dress does very nice things for you."

"Is that a compliment?"

"And you do even nicer things for the dress."

"Are you trying to make me blush?" Jillian asked as they passed the rows of people.

He grinned. "Is it working?"

"You're dangerous," she told him.

"Me? I'm harmless."

"Oh, no. I don't think you can be trusted for a minute."

"I can be trusted for lots of things," he countered as they reached the top of the aisle.

"Like what?"

His lips twitched as they reached the top of the aisle. "Let's get somewhere a little more private and I'd be happy to demonstrate."

"Oh, too bad we've got to go to the reception," Jillian said lightly. "I guess it'll have to wait." She was flirting, she realized in giddy wonder.

"I can be a pretty patient guy when I need to be," Gil returned.

And they walked through the front doors of the church into blazing sunlight and the pealing of the church's carillon.

The reception was at a lovely courtyard restaurant on the river. The June afternoon was mild enough to make it enjoyable, and if there was any flaw to it, it was that Jillian had been seated on the opposite side of the head table from Gil. That simmering sense of expectation still bubbled, even as she worked her way through appetizer and salad, soup and main course, making polite conversation with her companions, waiting for the moment she'd be free to talk with him again.

Because she had to admit it, she wanted to. She wanted to talk with him, to laugh with him, to hear his voice, to feel that little shiver in her stomach when she looked into his eyes.

When Lisa and Alan took the floor for their first dance, Jillian applauded with the rest, but mostly she was trying to manage the rush of anticipation and excitement and nerves. Because something had been set in motion. She had no better way to think about it than that. Something had changed from the night before—or maybe she had changed—and she had no idea what came next.

Except that she wanted more.

"All right, let's have the wedding party out on the floor for their dance," the band's lead singer said.

Jillian stood at the edge of the dance floor. For once in her life, she wasn't feeling tentative or uneasy or at loose ends. He'd come find her, she knew he would.

And then she turned and he was there.

"I think this is my dance," he said, offering her his hand.

Jillian stepped forward into his arms. The black fabric of his tux felt soft under her fingertips. She concentrated on that because it was safer than thinking about the way heat bloomed through her from his open hand pressed against her back, because that had her wondering just how that hand would feel smoothing over her skin. She shivered.

"Cold?" Gil murmured.

Jillian shook her head. How could she be, when she could feel the heat of his body just inches from hers? And even without that, there was the unsettling slide of his palm over hers, the disconcerting intimacy of having his mouth right at eye level, that delectable mouth that she found herself staring at even as she watched the corners of it turn up.

She raised her chin and found herself looking into his amused eyes.

"How am I doing?" he asked.

"Arthur Murray would be proud."

"Wait until I trot out my really smooth moves," he said.

"Is the world ready for that?"

"Come on, live life on the edge."

"How do you know I don't already?" she challenged. "I might be a daredevil."

"Running with scissors? Mixing whites with colors?"

"Skydiving," she countered. "Hang gliding. Bungee jumping."

"Bungee jumping?"

"Bungee jumping," she said triumphantly.

"Then this ought to feel familiar."

And before she knew what he was about, he'd tightened his hand at her waist and bent her backward into a deep dip.

A chorus of whoops erupted from the crowd around the dance floor. Jillian's heart hammered madly. He was bent over her, against her, pressing her tightly to him. And for a breathless, whirling instant, his mouth was almost touching hers.

Then he was standing her up again and bowing to the sounds of applause.

The edge, Jillian thought breathlessly, was getting closer by the moment.

The reception was over and the evening sky darkened to velvet black as Jillian and Gil walked out to the parking lot together. It was the first time she could remember that she'd danced until her feet ached. Now, she dangled her shoes from one hand and walked barefoot over the smooth pavement.

"So let me know if you want to go on tour with our dance-and-dip act," Gil told her.

"I'll have to take a look at my bungee jumping schedule," she said, stopping beside her car.

"You do that."

"Keep your smooth moves dusted off."

"Always do. You never know when you might need them." He studied her mouth. "You know, just because the wedding's over doesn't mean we have to go home. You want to go somewhere, get a drink?"

The idea appealed and alarmed. Taking a chance on him suddenly seemed like a far greater risk than merely jumping off a high platform. Yet the sense of anticipation that she'd felt all day suddenly intensified. "I'd like to but I'm meeting my brother and his family for breakfast early tomorrow."

"Lucky brother. Maybe some other time, then." She swallowed. "I'd like that."

"Yeah?" His eyes locked on hers. "So would I. Why don't you give me your number and I'll call you?"

She patted her small, beaded evening bag. "I don't have a pen or anything. Do you have something to write on?"

He shook his head. "Say it. I'll remember."

"You have a photographic memory?"

"For the important things." He reached out to trace his fingertips along her jaw.

Adrenaline surged through her. Her entire body, every nerve, every sense was immediately focused on that one place that his fingers touched. Warm, as they traced over her skin, just rough enough to give her gooseflesh. Her lips parted, seeking air.

"So tell me." Gil leaned in closer.

"Tell you?" she said blankly.

"Your number. You tell me and I'll repeat it." Jillian moistened her lips. "Two, two, five."

"Two, two, five." His gaze was hypnotic, overwhelming.

"Nine, three," she managed. Her heart thudded in her chest.

"Nine, three," he echoed.

Jillian hardly noticed when his arms slipped around her. "Two, one," she whispered. She could feel herself trembling. She caught a breath and found herself inhaling his air.

"Two, one," he murmured, his lips almost touching hers.

And then he kissed her.

Jillian had been kissed before. She knew what it was like to have a man's mouth on hers. It had never been *anything* like this. It had never set her entire body humming with pleasure. It had never made her forget everything around her, exist only for the mindless wonder of mouth on mouth.

Warm and wonderful and wicked, the kiss flowed through her with the delicious decadence of the most sinful dessert she could imagine. His mouth was softer than she'd expected, and clever, so clever, touching, tasting, tempting her lips to part. Her head fell back, her eyes fluttered shut and she clutched at his shoulders to keep her balance as his taste overwhelmed her.

She'd imagined how it would be with him, how his mouth would feel on hers. But nothing had prepared her for the overwhelming immediacy, for the tempting slide of tongue that had her knees weakening as desire flowed through her like some intoxicating drug that only had her wanting more. When she made a small, involuntary noise, she felt Gil's mouth curve against hers. His arms tightened around her, she could feel his body harden.

It exhilarated.

And it terrified. Without warning, her throat began to tighten up. Suddenly, she felt the old familiar panic, the one that had always dogged her, beginning to stir. Before she could protest, though, Gil released her. And then he was just smiling down at her and the panic was receding.

"Two, two, five, nine, three, two, one," he repeated and leaned in to kiss the tip of her nose. "I'll call you."

"If you get any more pregnant, Eric's going to have to rent a moving van to get you to the hospital," Jillian said to her sister-in-law, Jenny Logan, as they sat out on the back deck of the couple's house.

"Don't I know it. These Logan men are healthy individuals." Jenny leaned back on her chaise and rubbed one hand over her belly. "Why wasn't I smart enough to be attracted to a short man?"

"She keeps staring at me like it's my fault," Eric complained.

"Well, you were a part of the proceedings," Jenny pointed out.

"I had cooperation," he said. "Some very enthusiastic cooperation, as I recall."

"Too much information, guys," Jillian put in.

"Cole, you come away from that fence," Jenny directed her six-year-old adopted son.

Eric took two quick steps and hoisted the boy into the air before the rottweiler on the other side of the fence bounded up, barking. "Living life on the edge, my man."

"I can walk," Cole argued, squirming.

"No way," Eric said, tucking the boy under his arm as if he was a newspaper and tickling him until Cole giggled delightedly.

"So how was your wedding last night?" Jenny asked, a contented smile on her face. "Another dress for the horror museum?"

"No. Beautiful dress. Beautiful wedding. And…"

And a stupefyingly wonderful, all-time champion kiss.

Jenny gave her an interested look. "And?" she prompted.

"Nothing." Jillian flushed.

Eric was moving Cole through the air like Superman. "Look at Auntie Jillian turn tomato-red," he said.

"Tomato-red," Cole echoed gleefully.

"Nothing, eh?" Jenny observed. "I don't suppose this nothing happened to be a wedding guest, did he?"

"I think I hear the timer going off on the pastries," Jillian interrupted, hopping up.

"I'll help." Eric followed her into the house.

"You're going to have to answer my question sooner or later," Jenny called through the kitchen window.

Jillian pulled out the tray of bakery brioche and muffins she'd set to warm in the oven. "I can't hear you."

"You might as well give in," Eric advised as he poured coffee from the press pot into three mugs. "She's an expert at cross-examination."

That was the problem with a large family, Jillian thought. Nothing could ever remain a secret for long—sooner or later everything got out.

"He's just a man I met," she said offhandedly as she carried out the platter along with plates and napkins, Eric following.

"Not just a man," Jenny observed. "You like him."

"Okay, I like him. But it was just bridal-party stuff at the wedding. Who knows what'll come of it?"

"Do you want something to?" Jenny reached for the coffee mug Eric had set down before her.

"I want—"

"Cake!" Cole demanded, running up.

"Compromise," Eric said, handing him a mug of hot cocoa and a blueberry muffin.

"Hot chocolate!" Happily, Cole settled in with his muffin and drink.

"Gee, I didn't get any chocolate," Jenny said.

"Don't be so sure." Eric settled back with the paper.

Jenny took a sip. "Mocha!" she exclaimed. "Do you know how much I adore you?"

"Feel free to remind me," Eric said as he flipped open the paper.

Jillian shook her head at the *Gazette.* "You know, I'm torn every time I see that rag," she pronounced, breaking the little ball off the top of her brioche. "Half of me wants to burn it and the other half is desperately curious to pick it up to see if they've printed any new trash about Robbie." As if driving him away hadn't been enough.

"Don't give yourself ulcers over it," Eric said. "That first story was a little strong but they've been better since."

"Sure. Now they want a comment from him. Now that he's gone. Or maybe they're just sniffing around for a new story."

"They don't really have to. The tabloids have kind of taken it over."

And it drove Jillian nuts. One day Robbie had been there, the next he'd been gone without a word. One letter, no phone calls. Five weeks. She shook her head. "It's driving Nancy to distraction, especially since he's supposed to be checking in with his parole officer."

"I don't know how she's managing. I can't imagine how I'd feel if Eric just disappeared like that," Jenny said. "I'd be worried out of my mind."

"She is. I just keep hoping it'll all die down, but fat chance." Jillian leaned back in her chair, staring at the paper that hid Eric. "It's just one story after another after anoth—" Suddenly, she froze, staring at the banner. The *Portland Gazette,* it read. And on the line below, in fancy script, A Blazon Media Company.

A Blazon Media company.

"What's wrong?" Jenny asked, frowning. "You look like you'd seen a ghost."

"Eric, can I have the front page for a minute?"

"Hmm?"

"The front page. Just for a minute. Here, you can have the sports section." She took the opening section with shaking hands. "Come on, come on, come on," she muttered.

"You mind telling me what's going on?" Eric asked.

"Nothing." It didn't mean anything, she told herself as she turned back to the editorial page, the part that carried the masthead. Just because Blazon owned the paper didn't mean Gil worked for the *Gazette.* He could do any one of a number of things. Maybe he was in corporate, maybe he was in radio. Maybe he handled their Internet properties.

Or maybe, just maybe, he was the managing editor for the metro section of the *Gazette*.

"I'm going to strangle him," Jillian said.

Chapter Four

He was staring into space again, Gil realized with a start. Looking aimlessly out the window at the lights along the Willamette River. And seeing a pair of whiskey-colored eyes, for the umpteenth time since he'd watched Jillian Logan drive away on Saturday night.

It wasn't like him to let a woman get into his head like this. Sure, he'd been attracted before. He'd even been wildly in lust a few times. Love? Not really his thing. He did better with like. He was one of those guys who liked women through and through, the way they looked, the way they smelled, the way they walked and talked and dressed and blushed. The way they were all different. He liked taking them out, he liked taking them to bed.

And he liked having his life to himself after it was over.

So why did he have Jillian Logan stuck in his head? He kept remembering that husky laugh of hers, that way she had of staying two steps ahead of him, of keeping him on his toes the way almost nobody did. And those soft little gasps she'd made when they were kissing, her hand curled into the front of his shirt as though she couldn't get enough. Those soft little gasps that had kept him thinking quite a lot about what was underneath that pretty purple dress of hers. If it had just been him and her somewhere private, he might have started to find out.

But it wasn't just him and her, that was the problem. She was Jillian Logan, the sister of Robbie Logan of the Children's Connection scandal. And he was the city editor of the *Gazette*. Alan had warned him of that going into the wedding, Gil reminded himself. He'd known ahead of time to keep his distance.

He just hadn't been able to help himself.

So now he had a fine mess on his hands. He was the editor of the paper that had outed Robbie Logan and touched off a media firestorm. Considering how protective Jillian had been over Lisa when Gil had missed the rehearsal, he had a pretty good idea that she was going to be seriously ticked when she found out.

Add to that the fact that he'd told her he was with Blazon Media instead of the paper, which only made it look as though he was trying to hide it. That was far from the case, but how would she know?

Letting out a long breath, Gil drummed his fingers on the arm of his couch. He had to be straight with her, that was all there was to it. If he wanted to see where things between them could go, he had to come clean. He'd take her out to dinner, somewhere with good wine and quiet music and lay it all out for her. She'd be angry at first, maybe— okay, definitely—but once she'd had some time to think about it, there was a good chance she'd get past it. After all, the paper was only doing its job, reporting the facts. The public had a right to know. Gil believed that through and through.

The question was, would Jillian?

She'd never been much good at meditating. Oh, sure, she had all the yoga poses down, but as she eased into the triangle, standing on her living-room carpet, Jillian's thoughts coalesced like bits of mercury, flowing together in fits and starts.

Until she was thinking of Gil Reynolds once again.

He worked for the *Gazette,* the paper that had driven Robbie away. Maybe he hadn't written the articles himself, but as editor he might as well have. And the worst part about it was that he'd lied to her. *Lied* to her. Blazon Media her ass. He'd only said it because he'd known who she was, and known she'd go off on him if he told her the truth.

Instead, she'd kissed him. She'd stood in the parking lot and glommed onto him like a limpet. And made it totally clear she'd liked it. Forget like, she'd loved it, and he'd known. She remembered the feel of his mouth curving against hers and she suddenly had a new appreciation for the phrase *seeing red* because she swore she could see the ruddy haze of anger like a fine mist over everything in her view.

A dozen flavors of fury, humiliation, betrayal layered over one another, and underneath, deep underneath lurked a dark, sneaky disappointment. It had felt so right. This was the one that she'd thought was actually going to work, the one that was going to happen the way it did for everyone else, meeting a guy, going out and, who knew, maybe getting involved, maybe even, God forbid, having sex for once in her life. It wasn't too much to ask for, was it? Was it?

Instead, she'd gotten Gil Reynolds playing his tricky game and probably laughing at her the entire time.

Relax, Jillian reminded herself, taking a deep breath as she changed sides and sank back into the pose. Exercise was supposed to soothe, not give her a chance to get more agitated.

The worst part was that she'd liked him, really liked him. He'd seemed genuinely interested, as though he'd been attracted to her, wanted her. What if he hadn't been?

What if he'd only been trying to pump her for a story?

And at that thought, all possibility of relaxation flew out the window. Forget yoga, she needed to learn something more violent. Kickboxing, maybe, something where she could hit and kick and...

Release, she reminded herself. Let it go.

The phone burbled. Jillian struggled out of her pose and made it over to the handset. As a social worker, answering the phone was never optional for her.

"Hello?"

"Jillian? Gil Reynolds."

Let it go? Not likely. "Why, Gil," she said silkily, "what a coincidence. I was just thinking about you."

"Great minds," he said. "Having a good week?"

"All right. How about you?"

"Ah, keeping busy."

"Oh, I just bet you are," she said.

He stopped a moment. "Yeah. Well." He cleared his throat. "I was wondering if you still wanted to get together. How about dinner tomorrow night? I was hoping we could talk."

"We can talk now."

"Face-to-face is a lot more fun," he said. "Come on, let me buy you dinner."

"How about lunch?" she countered. He was right, face-to-face was a lot more fun, and she couldn't wait to see his when she dropped the bombshell. "Let's go somewhere downtown," she added.

"All right. How about noon at Conroy's?"

"Great. I'll meet you there."

"I'm looking forward to it," he said.

Not nearly as much as she was, Jillian thought grimly as she hung up the phone.

"Reynolds. My office, five minutes." Russell Gleason, the *Gazette*'s publisher, barked the words through Gil's open door.

"I've got—" Gil began but he was already gone. Gil bit back a curse. He was supposed to be leaving for lunch with Jillian, not sitting in a meeting all afternoon. And with Russ, you never knew. The discussion could last five minutes. It could just as easily last an hour and forty-five, depending on how many tangents he wandered off on.

The topic was sales and circulation. Or, more to the point, what Gleason thought they ought to do to editorial to provide him with better sales and circ.

Like controversy.

"I'm just saying, we need stories that sell."

"Stories that sell?" Gil stared at Gleason. "We've just lit a big enough fire under Nash and his cronies that the state's threatening an audit. What more do you want?"

The publisher tapped his fingers on the black slab of his desk, dissatisfaction coming off him in waves. "That's politics. That doesn't sell papers in this day and age. We need something juicier."

"Politics doesn't sell papers? This is Portland we're talking about. People here live and breathe politics. Take a look at your reader surveys."

"All I know is when you broke the story about that football player's kid, our newsstand numbers went through the roof."

Gil bristled. "First of all, I didn't break that story. I was on vacation when it hit. And if you remember, we had to print a retraction on parts of it. Sloppy researching, sloppy editing and it was just your pure damned good luck that Lisa Sanders didn't take legal action." And that he hadn't lost one of his closest friends over it, Gil added silently.

"There wasn't anything actionable," Gleason scoffed, but his eyes flickered.

"Look, Russ, you take care of the business end and let me deal with editorial. Separation of church and state, right?"

"I'm just saying we've got stuff going on around here. What about that Logan thing?"

"I've got Mark Fetzer on it."

"So why haven't I seen any more stories?"

"They have to do something before we can write about it," Gil reminded him wearily.

"Look at that *Weekly Messenger.* They run a Logan story on the front page just about every issue."

"When they're not writing about Elvis sightings. Russ, for Christ's sake, the *Messenger* is a tabloid. They don't need facts, they print tripe. We're Portland's primary newspaper. We've got a responsibility."

"Yeah, to our advertisers and shareholders. I want Logans," Gleason said obstinately. "That family sells newspapers. Besides, it's a public service. With all the fiascos that clinic has had, it should be shut down."

"Funny, the state and federal regulators don't agree with you."

"Yeah, well, our state senator does."

"Showboating." Gil dismissed it. "Look, it's not our role. Our role is to support the news."

"Our *role* is to support our shareholders," Gleason countered.

"Circulation was just fine the last time I checked. And ad sales. In fact, I seem to remember cutting a story last week because the ad count ran over. You do what you do well, Russ, and leave me to what I do well. Look—" Gil checked his watch "—can we get back on this in the afternoon? I've got a lunch meeting."

"Skip your lunch meeting. Go ask Nash what he thinks about a babynapper running a day care center. Better yet, go interview a Logan."

Gil snorted and rose. "Yeah, sure, Russ. I'll get right on that."

She had to give it to him, he'd chosen well. It was a quiet little restaurant in the Pearl District. Once, the area had been home to light industry, auto-repair garages and the like. No, it had become fashionable, the welding shops and upholstery businesses supplanted by galleries and expensive boutiques, hair salons and intimate restaurants whose tabs rose in indirect proportion to the number of tables.

Gil hadn't chosen one of the chichi ones, though, but a modest little pub that might well have been there the whole time. It was quiet and only half full. Privacy, Jillian thought as she glanced at her watch. They'd be able to have their conversation without having to shout to be heard. Which was fine with her. Scenes had never been her thing. She wanted answers. She wanted to know why the *Gazette* had gone after Robbie. She wanted to know why Gil had lied. And she'd find out.

Provided he ever bothered to show up.

Stifling impatience, she took a sip of water and set the glass precisely back in its damp ring. She'd arrived her habitual five minutes early. Now fifteen more had gone by and she itched to check voice mail, to drag out her PDA, do something productive with the time. But she didn't. She had a personal rule about waving electronics around in restaurants. Then again, if Gil didn't show up soon, she might just break that rule.

Or walk out entirely.

When she glanced over to the door again, though, he was there. And for a moment, her thoughts scattered. For a moment, she was back in the church at the head of the aisle and he was watching her every step. Except this time around, she was the one watching. The man had presence, she'd give him that. There was something absolutely riveting about him. She wasn't the only one who thought so; she saw a waitress turn to stare in his wake.

Jillian just gazed, unmoving, until he was standing beside the table, looking down at her.

"Hello," he said. She hated the fact that her pulse stuttered. He hesitated a moment, long enough that, for a breathless instant, she wondered if he was going to lean down and kiss her.

But he didn't. Instead, he sat. "Sorry I'm late. My boss called me in just as I was leaving."

"Trouble?"

His grin flashed, quick and white. "No more than usual."

Just looking at him made her remember the feel of his mouth on hers, the taste of him, the intimacy of that dark, male flavor. And the man knew how to kiss, knew how to use that clever, clever mouth to turn a woman to mush.

Not her, not anymore, she reminded herself grimly.

"So how was the rest of your weekend? Breakfast with your brother, right?"

"Good memory," she said.

"Where'd you go?"

"His house. His wife's pregnant and on bed rest, so I brought the breakfast. We mostly just sat outside, drank coffee. And read the paper," she added, watching him closely. "After all, it wouldn't be Sunday without the paper, would it?"

"No, indeed. Are you a big newspaper fan?" he asked, just a touch of care in his words.

"Oh, about like average. I like to know what's going on in town. Of course, I like it from a reputable paper, not a scandal rag."

"Don't like reading about Brangelina and space aliens?" He looked amused.

"Don't like seeing people's reputations trashed. Some of these reporters, they're like snipers taking potshots from deep cover. They stay nice and safe while they destroy innocent people's lives. And the editors just let them do it."

"Not everybody who winds up in the paper is innocent."

"And not every story written is accurate. Of course, the problem is that the jazzy stories show up on page one and the retractions show up on the bottom corner of page thirty-eight."

"News sells."

"Wrecking people's lives sells," she countered.

Gil leaned forward. "So did Woodward and Bernstein destroy lives or uncover corruption in government?"

"Not every reporter out there is working for the greater good. Or every newspaper."

"It's not all heroes and villains, you know."

"On either side. The world's not black-and-white. Trust me, I know that." She gave a short laugh. "But I think I got us off on a tangent here. Enough of that. Tell me how life's going at Blazon Media," she said casually. "Or should I say the *Portland Gazette?* That is where you work, right? The *Portland Gazette?*"

Nailed, Gil thought. When he'd been a kid, he'd been at a pet shop one time when the owner put a mouse in the snake tank for a rattler to eat. He remembered watching the mouse edge around in the corner, knowing that something was up but not knowing quite what, only knowing that things didn't feel right. And then quick as lightning, the snake had struck.

Like Jillian.

"Okay." He exhaled. "You're probably pretty ticked right now and I don't blame you. Yes, I work for the *Gazette,* which is owned by Blazon. And yes, I'm the city editor."

"The city editor. The one responsible for all the Portland stories on the front page. Like the stories on my brother." She'd clasped her hands together calmly, setting them on the table before her. Only, he could see that her knuckles were white.

Gil let out a breath slowly. "I know how this looks," he began. "I brought you here so that I could te—"

"Why did you lie to me last weekend?" she interrupted.

He closed his eyes briefly. "For the same reason we're having this conversation now. The focus was supposed to be on the bride and groom. It wasn't about you and me and the issues you might have with my newspaper. It was their day, not ours. And they wanted us both there."

She opened her mouth and closed it. "You could have told me the other night, over the phone."

"I didn't want to do it over the phone. That's why I called and asked you out, I wanted to do it face-to-face. I wanted to get it right."

She snorted. "Why start now? Accuracy hasn't exactly been your hallmark the past three months while you've been dragging my brother's name through the mud."

"We've been covering a story," he corrected tightly. "And I insist on rigorous fact-checking."

"Oh, is that what you call it? Like the way you did with Lisa's story? I can't believe she'd even have you in her wedding."

Gil's jaw tightened. "The story about Lisa happened off my watch and I fixed it when I got home. As to your brother, it's all been accurate. We're a newspaper, Jillian. It's our job to cover the news."

"And if you can sell a few more papers with a flashy headline, so much the better."

He ruthlessly tamped down the frustration. She was upset and she was striking out. "Look, I'm sorry your family's been hurt and I'm sorry for any problems Robbie has faced but I still think the public has a right to know."

"A right to know?" she echoed incredulously.

Now it was his turn to be irritated. "That a baby-napper's running a day care center? Yeah, I do."

Her eyes flashed. "You don't know anything about it. You never bothered to find out, never called us for a comment."

"The reporter tried twice. I saw the phone logs. There was no comment. We had to run the story."

"Along with a few quotes from politicians looking to make headlines."

"And quotes from the state regulatory groups when they decided the situation was fine as it was," he reminded her.

"Oh, sure, on page thirty-eight."

"No, page three, actually."

"Do you think that changed anything?" she demanded. "Nobody noticed, nobody remembered. The tabloids already had their meat by then."

He raised his hands in frustration. "All I can control is what's in my pages. I can't control what the tabloids do."

"No, you just throw out the juicy bone and stand back and watch them tear at it like a pack of hounds. That doesn't make you less of a scavenger." Two spots of color burned high on her cheeks.

"It's not personal, Jillian, don't you understand? What the paper does is never personal, it can't be." But he saw the betrayal in her eyes. Gil took a deep breath and let it out slowly. "Let's not do this, okay? We had something at the wedding, before this came up. Back when we were just people, something clicked."

"And it was a lie."

"No. I'm still me, you're still you, whatever's going on around us. And I don't want to lose this without trying."

"Do you honestly think I would in a million years be involved with you after what you've done?" she asked incredulously. "Do you think I want anything to do with you, at all?"

"Jillian, it's not about us."

"Of *course* it's about us, Gil," she retorted. "It's all about us. You can't break life up into neat little compartments. This is my family you're talking about, my job, a clinic that saved my brother and me. And I don't care if you and your paper aren't writing the stories now, you're responsible for it."

"So, what, all the sins of the media are laid at my feet?"

"When you deserve them, yes."

"No. This isn't over. I'm not walking away from this."

"Fine," she snapped. "Then I'll do it." And she rose.

Jillian strode down the sidewalk, fuming. How could he be so clueless as to think it didn't matter? To sit there and tell her it was his job to dog Robbie with old mistakes, to trot out the traumas he'd suffered and make him live them over and over? To try to tell her—tell everyone—that he was broken and would never be right again?

She sucked in a breath of air because it was either that or scream. It was so unfair, so incredibly unfair. To have him sit there and try to justify it all to her just made her crazy. And to have him tell her that he'd felt something for her was bitter, indeed.

Because she'd felt something for him.

But it was a lie, all of it, a lie she had to forget.

Just as she had to forget him. Forget how it had been to spar with him at the rehearsal dinner, forget walking down the aisle, forget dancing in his arms, staring into those eyes.

And forget the kiss above all, the promise, the passion, that sense that she'd been standing on the edge of something she'd never before experienced in her life.

She was done with him. Not only did he work for the *Gazette,* he'd lied to her about it. No matter how he'd tried to justify it, he'd lied and taken advantage of her belief. So he was gone? She was glad of it. She wasn't just letting him go, she was walking away. And she was going to keep walking. Mark Gil Reynolds *D* for done. It was over and she was happy about it.

So why were her eyelids prickling?

Gil stalked across the editorial floor of the *Gazette,* his mood unbelievably foul.

"Tom in graphics needs to get your okay on the streetcar art," Lynn, his admin, said as he walked by.

"Later," he said.

"And Russ wants to talk to you—"

"Later," he snapped, and slammed his office door behind him, leaving her staring in his wake. Perfect. Now he'd owe Lynn an apology for his uncharacteristic outburst. If he'd been smart, he'd have taken the afternoon off rather than subject anyone to dealing with him.

Dammit to hell, Jillian had found out, she'd found out before he could tell her. And maybe he should have been straight with her from the very beginning but he'd made a promise.

"Look," Alan had said over beers at the Lucky Lab a few weeks before, "Lisa and I argued for three hours last night about whether you were going to be in the wedding and it was a near, near thing."

"Hey, three hours of arguing and you're still getting married?" Gil had taken a swallow of his pint of IPA. "Sounds like I gave you two a chance to see how you handle conflict."

"This isn't funny. Lisa feels like she owes a lot to Jillian. It's important to her that Jillian's in the wedding."

And as a Logan, Jillian would consider anyone from the *Gazette* as the Antichrist. Gil could figure that much without trying. "Come on, Alan, we're all grown-ups. It's okay if you need to take back your invitation. It's cool. I understand. I mean, I'm deeply, deeply hurt, but I'll get over it. Especially if you get those Trailblazers season tickets you've been talking about and take me to half the games with you."

"Forget it."

"A quarter of them?" Gil had asked hopefully.

"I mean, forget it about crying off. I want you standing up with me. We go back. You weren't in my first wedding. Nobody was. I want to do it right this time."

However much Alan had made his peace with dropping out of college when he'd gotten his girlfriend pregnant at twenty-one, Gil knew that their friendship had remained a talisman of sorts, a memory for Alan of carefree days that had ended too soon.

"Look, I appreciate the thought, but if it's going to cause a problem with Lisa and her friend, it's not worth it. I'll sit out in the audience and wave to you."

"You'll be there. Just remember, you work for Blazon Media, not the *Gazette*."

"Wait a minute. I'm not crazy about—"

"It's only for the rehearsal and the wedding," Alan had interrupted. "After that, you'll never see her again."

Only, it hadn't turned out that way. Instead, the temporary stopgap had turned into a nice little bomb that had blown up in his face. Frustration boiled through him. It hadn't been his idea. More to the point, there had been nothing wrong with the *Gazette*'s coverage. They weren't responsible for what the rest of the media did, but the public had a right to know. He believed that through and through.

His mistake hadn't been coverage, his mistake had been strategy: Going along with the Blazon idea and then not confessing to Jillian at first opportunity. He should have told her when he'd called, but no, he'd wanted to be cute and do it face-to-face, where he'd be most persuasive. And he definitely should have told her the minute he'd gotten to the restaurant. Except that it had felt good, just sitting and talking as though there was no shadow over them.

Too bad he couldn't pretend there wasn't one.

There was something else there between them, though, a connection that he wasn't ready to walk away from. And there was no way he was going to let her walk away from it, either. There was a way to make it work; he just had to figure it out.

Tapping the desktop thoughtfully, he picked up his phone. "Hey, Lynn, can you get me Dana in the Portland-Works section?"

Chapter Five

"Jillian! Just the person I was looking for. Got five minutes?"

Jillian glanced up through the tendril of steam rising from her mug of tea to see her cousin LJ leaning in her office door.

Cousins. She had cousins now. Incredible to think that after years of estrangement between her adoptive father Terrence and his brother Lawrence, the two families were back in touch.

Ostensibly, the two brothers had fallen out over a pair of self-help books that Lawrence had written on families, which included thinly veiled examples from Terrence's life. Jillian hadn't needed a master's degree in social work to understand that the roots went much deeper, though: well-hidden, fiercely denied insecurities that caused both men to look for slights from one another even as they indulged in self-congratulation that edged toward bravado.

Family dynamics, Jillian thought with a sigh. Without them, she wouldn't have a job. With them, though, she'd felt like a fraud—the woman who counseled families while her own was divided by a rift wider than the Grand Canyon.

It had been a matter of purest chance, really, that things had changed. If she hadn't gone to the health-care conference in Seattle and seen a Dr. Jake Logan on the program, it would never have happened. But she *had* gone, and approaching Lawrence's son Jake had been the first of a series of gradual changes like a slow, ponderous chain reaction that had resulted in a tentative reconciliation between her father and her uncle.

And given her a whole other side of the family to learn about: not just Jake, but his brothers Scott and Ryan, his stepsisters Suzie and Janet. And LJ, whom she regarded now with amusement.

"Do you all have to look so much alike?" she complained. "You ought to wear name badges. A person could get completely confused."

"Not at all," he said, stepping into the room and

dropping into one of her chairs. "Look for the best-dressed guy in the room and it'll be me."

"Big words from a man who left his Armani at home this morning."

"It's after Memorial Day. *Esquire* says it's linen time."

She glanced at his olive shirt and wheat trousers. "If you ever wanted to give up marketing and PR, I bet you could make a tidy living as a model, *Esquire* boy."

"I'd rather keep my gifts on the small stage."

"Your modesty is so becoming."

He grinned. "Isn't it, though? Is that coffee?" he asked as she lifted her mug and took a drink.

"Tea. Chamomile," Jillian added. "It's very soothing. Want some?" She'd been mainlining it since her lunch with Gil three days before. Not that it had helped much.

LJ gave her a disgusted look. "Uh, no. I'll skip soothing and go straight for the High Test."

"Your choice."

"Thankfully."

She wrinkled her nose at him. "So how's the bicoastal life working out?" Two months before, LJ had been a committed New Yorker with a thriving PR business. Then, while he'd been out to do an image overhaul of the Children's Connection, the clinic's doula, Eden Carter, along with her younger son, Liam, had spun his world right around. Now, he was in love, in deep, and busily moving to Portland a bit at a time.

"I'm here with Eden and Liam this week. Life is good."

"Are you ever going to make an honest woman out of her? I mean, granted you're bringing your business out and the two of you have moved in together, but it's not the real deal, is it?"

"I'm working on it. Eden wants to wait for the wedding until everything's settled back East."

"Is that what you want?"

He grinned. "Have some faith. I've just been waiting to bring out the lethal charm until the time was right. In the meantime, I've bought the rock."

"The rock?"

"Tanzanite, to match her eyes. Any loser can get a diamond. I've got a custom jeweler just waiting to make her a setting. All I need to do is drag her in to see him. But that wasn't why I stopped by."

"Oh, right, I was supposed to get you my recommendations for the new recruiting brochure, wasn't I?" Yet another action item she'd let fall off her list. She'd been doing that a lot the past few days.

"I do need your input but this is more about PR for the clinic itself."

"We can't possibly have enough of that."

"I'm gratified to hear that you think so," LJ said

smoothly. "We've got an opportunity to run a piece that'll put the focus on the clinic's services and some of its success stories."

"Excellent. Count on me to help any way I can."

"Well, actually you're a key part of it." He adjusted his cuffs. "*The* key part of it, a person might say."

Jillian set her tea down slowly. "*The* key part?"

"I've got a publication that wants to profile you for their employment section. You know, a day in the life of a social worker? Although they'd have to shadow you for a week to really get the full picture."

"LJ, I've got sessions," she protested, "closed-door meetings. They can't shadow me."

"Not all the time, but enough to get a picture of what you do and maybe interview the clients who are open to it. We need this, Jillian."

Just the idea made her uncomfortable. "They've got to follow me around? They can't just interview me?"

"That wouldn't give them enough information for their format."

She frowned. "What's the publication?"

He coughed. "The *Portland Gazette*."

Jillian stared at him. "The *Portland Gazette?* Are you out of your mind? They've taken every opportunity they can to trash the Children's Connection. They tore Lisa to bits when her birth father showed up spreading lies and now they've driven Robbie away. And you want to work with them?"

"Actually, yes."

His calm answer took some of the wind out of her sails. "Would you mind clarifying that for me?"

"We need the good press, Jillian. They can do things for us. We don't have to like them to benefit from them."

"What makes you think they won't send someone who'll twist everything out of shape?" she demanded. "Don't you see? They're coming in to dig up more dirt. What if they find out Robbie's gone? If his probation officer finds out, he'll be in violation. And being gone makes him look guilty."

"Guilty of what?"

"Whatever they want, once the tabloids get hold of it."

"First of all, I'd defy anyone to spend five days with you here and come away with anything but positive output. Second, this is a job profile, not a news piece. They run one every Sunday, starting on the front page and jumping to the employment section. I've read the series. They're universally positive. The reporter guarantees it will focus on your work, not on the clinic. And I trust him."

"You trust him? Who is—" And suddenly it all clicked. "Oh, no."

"What?"

"No—" she shook her head "—it's Gil Reynolds, isn't it?"

"You know him?"

"I know him, all right, and this doesn't have a lick to do with my work. This has to do with—" She stopped abruptly.

LJ gave her an interested smile. "This has to do with?" he prompted.

"Nothing," she muttered. She wasn't about to unveil her ridiculous private life to LJ. Or what passed for a private life for her, anyway. "How can you possibly want to work with him? He approved all those stories on Robbie."

"I know," he soothed. "But the *Gazette*'s a reputable paper. So they dropped the bomb on the Children's Connection and Robbie. If they turn around and carry a story that plugs the clinic, it'll carry that much more weight."

"And what if the tabloid vultures come swooping in?"

"We can't control what the tabloids do, Jillian. The *Gazette* can be our ally, if we let it. What helps the Children's Connection helps Robbie."

"You're putting me in a corner, LJ."

"Of course I am. And for the sake of the clinic, I'd do a lot more. In this business, you work with who you need to, not who you like.

Come on, Jillian," he coaxed, "do it for your favorite cousin?"

She glowered at him. "All right," she said finally.

"Great." He rose.

"You know, when I'd said you were my favorite cousin, I lied."

"Drink some more of your tea," LJ advised. "I've heard it's calming." Whistling, he walked out of the room.

It was absolutely infuriating. A job profile, her foot. The whole scheme had nothing to do with jobs—it had to do with Gil Reynolds being constitutionally incapable of taking no for an answer. He was a guy who'd always gotten exactly what he wanted without earning it, she diagnosed, one who'd never had to work because everything fell in his lap. And because she wasn't dropping for him, he'd concocted this ridiculous scheme in a blatant attempt to get past her guard.

Which she hoped to God he couldn't do. No way did she want Gil Reynolds in her head—bad enough he was already popping up in her dreams. Not that that was anything other than her subconscious processing anxiety, she reassured herself. It had nothing to do with actually wanting him. She didn't know what wanting even was. Even the sex dreams she'd had about him were incomplete. One minute, they'd be kissing and clinching and she'd know—she'd *know*—that this was it. The next, he'd disappear, leaving her confused and wanting.

The same way he would probably disappear in real life if she told him she was a virgin at thirty-three. She was fully aware of just how freakish that was. And every year that went by, the thought of looking at a potential lover and confiding her secret was more daunting.

Not that it even mattered in this case. She was not about to let Gil Reynolds get to her. He'd already come after Lisa and Robbie with the *Gazette*. He wasn't going to get his chance with Jillian.

Suddenly, her chamomile tea wasn't remotely appealing. She needed something more. Rising, she stomped down the hall and over the land bridge to the break room in the hospital across the street. Chocolate. She knew it was only a crutch, but dammit, it was a crutch she needed.

She'd been neatly boxed in. She didn't even want to speak with Gil, let alone have him glued to her hip for a week.

Glued to her hip.

That brought up way too many images she just didn't want to deal with. Instead, she debated the merits of chomping nuts in a Snickers or crisps in a Kit Kat, finally electing to pass on both in favor of mainlining a Dove bittersweet chocolate bar.

Bittersweet. That about said it.

"You're not looking happy."

She turned to see Eden Carter standing behind her, all gorgeous and curvy and blond.

"Would you take it personally if I strangled the love of your life?" Jillian asked.

"Since he just got in about two hours ago and we haven't had sex yet, yes," Eden replied. "At least let me get in an orgasm or two, first."

"He's out of his mind." Jillian stabbed the button that released her candy bar.

"He mentioned that you were a little upset."

"Do you know what he wants me to do?" Jillian demanded. "Work with the *Gazette*. That paper's been after us for years and he wants me to make nice with them."

"News is news," Eden said philosophically, feeding coins into the machine to get a package of fruit bites. "Give them a good story instead of something negative and maybe you can undo some of the damage."

"That's what LJ says."

"And as much as it fries me to admit it, the man is usually right. Of course, if you tell him I said that, I'll deny it to my dying breath."

"Why couldn't it be someone else?" Okay, so she was whining but wasn't she allowed to once in a while?

"I don't imagine anyone could come off as well

as you do. You're tops at your profession. You make people's lives better and you never get ruffled. There's no way that reporter's ever going to get you to say the wrong thing."

If anyone could, Jillian reflected, it was probably Gil Reynolds.

"Jillian, trust LJ," Eden said. "We need all the help we can get."

"I suppose," Jillian said.

"I know." Eden slung an arm around Jillian's shoulders. "Anyway, it's only a week. How bad can it be?"

She should have stayed and worked at bringing her notes up to date, Jillian knew. After staring into space for half an hour, though, it was clear to her that she wasn't going to get anything done. She needed some peace to stop her mind from going in circles and she wasn't going to get it in her office.

Jillian had never used the generous trust fund her parents had established for each of their children, preferring to make her own way in the world. The one exception was the money she'd drawn out for a down payment on her home in the Ladd's Addition neighborhood of Portland. She barely remembered the first four years of her life, the ones where she didn't have a home, but they'd been subtly encoded in her makeup. She craved security and she'd found it in the green-shingled Craftsman bungalow with its broad, welcoming front porch and dormer windows.

She'd bought it at twenty-five after grad school, when she'd jumped into the working world. It had been a labor of love, from the furniture and floors she'd refinished to the garden she lovingly tended. Working on it was her own form of meditation. It was the one place she truly felt safe.

And so she went to the garden and talked to the azaleas and rhododendrons and lilacs, plants that were like old friends, each of them known by face and by name. Barefoot, in shorts and a T-shirt, she pulled weeds, thinned the carrots in the vegetable garden. She watered the tomatoes, hot peppers and tomatillos in her salsa garden and admired the fuchsias that had begun to bloom in her hanging baskets. With shears, she cut some sweet pea blossoms to go into the old milk bottle that sat on her kitchen table.

"I thought I might find you here."

Jillian jumped and whirled around to see a tall man with thick, undisciplined dark hair walk up.

"God, don't *ever* come up behind me like that. Next time make some noise so you don't scare the life out of me." She pressed a hand to her chest.

"You're my twin. Aren't you supposed to know I'm around?"

David Logan, her brother by blood, the only one she truly dropped the barriers with. David, the one who knew nearly all of her secrets.

She leaned in to give him a hug. "Sorry, my twin detector is out of batteries. I can offer you a beer, though, if you don't mind getting it yourself. I'll wash these." She held up her dirty hands.

"You want one?"

"I'll take an iced tea, please." After what had happened the last time she'd tried drinking, she'd stick with teetotaling.

It should have seemed like an uncanny coincidence that David had shown up when she was upset. Somehow, though, he always knew. The normal rules didn't apply with either of them. If anyone else had stopped over unexpectedly, she'd have been rattled and uncomfortable. Not with David, though. Never with David. And even if things had changed once he'd married and gotten a family, there was a connection there she'd never had with any other person.

For all she knew, it was part of why she found it so hard to meet men. Not that she was hung up on her brother but that some part of her craved that bone-deep connection the two of them had always shared. Anything else just wasn't enough.

"So what brings you by?" she asked as he brought the bottles back out, along with a bag of habanero potato chips he'd scavenged.

He shrugged. "I dunno, I was just in the neighborhood and figured I'd stop by. It's been a couple of weeks."

Together, they sat in the green-painted Adirondack chairs on her back deck.

"Any word from Robbie?" David asked.

Jillian surveyed her garden and willed it to give her peace. "Just the one letter right after he disappeared. Nancy's going out of her mind. And she's terrified every time the phone rings that it's going to be his probation officer."

"I can imagine. If I weren't so worried about him I'd be tempted to strangle him."

"If you could find him."

"I could find him," he said with the quiet certainty of a State Department special agent. "Just like Scott will find him." Scott Logan, their cousin, the private investigator searching for Robbie. "That doesn't excuse Robbie running out. Marriage is supposed to be about being there for each other."

"David, come on, this isn't a normal situation. He was kidnapped at what, six? When a child experiences trauma that young, the scars are incredibly deep. I mean, it's bad enough he was taken, but to have those people brainwashing him, telling him Mom and Dad didn't want him? You don't get over that kind of thing in a year or two of therapy. You don't get over it in decades."

"We did."

Had they? "We were lucky. Six was when the bad stuff ended for us. For Robbie, it was just beginning."

"He knows the real score now."

"And knowing intellectually isn't the same thing as *knowing,*" she responded. "Trust me on that. He was doing better, I know he was. And he was happy with Nancy. But he wasn't ready to have everything dredged back up by the paper. He wasn't ready to have all his mistakes rubbed in his face."

"Being involved in a babynapping ring is a pretty big mistake."

"I know." Her voice was impatient. "But he was forced into it and he did the right thing in the end. Doesn't he get some credit for that? Doesn't he get some credit for the good he's done? When does he get to leave it all behind?"

"You never leave anything behind. It's always with you. It's just a question of whether you let it ride you."

She raised her eyebrows. "Keep it up and we might just make a social worker out of you, yet."

"My dream job," he said drily.

"Oh, speaking of jobs, wait until you hear the latest."

"About being a social worker?"

"Sort of. It's your cousin LJ's fault."

David's lips twitched. "*My* cousin?"

"He is when he's being annoying. And right now he's being really annoying. He's cooked up some agreement to have the *Gazette* do a profile on me for their careers section. The reporter's going to shadow me all week next week."

"Cool. We'll finally get some good press out of that paper for a change."

She stared at him. What was with everyone? "Easy for you to say. You're not the one who's going to have a jerk reporter breathing down your neck all week. Oh, I bet he's so pleased with himself," she muttered darkly.

David looked puzzled. "LJ?"

"Gil Reynolds. The reporter who cooked it all up," she elaborated. "And he is so going to be sorry."

David raised an eyebrow. "You know this guy?"

"I met him at a friend's wedding." And kissed his face off. "Before I knew he worked for the *Gazette*."

"Before you knew he was the Evil Other?"

She shot a look at him from under her brows. "I'd appreciate a little support here. That paper went after our family."

"He wrote the stories?"

"He might as well have. He was the editor who approved them."

"So maybe he feels bad and wants to give the clinic some good press."

"He's a journalist, David. He's not doing it because he feels bad, he's doing it because he wasn't getting his way."

David took a swallow of beer. "Seems to me like you're pretty hostile about this guy. And I get the feeling that it's not all about him working for the paper."

Trust David to go unerringly to the heart of anything bugging her.

Even if she didn't want to talk about it.

"So, how are Liz and the kids?" she asked briskly.

"Whoa. Way to change the subject."

"The subject was done."

"So you jumped from talking about your reporter guy to talking about my wife and kids. Interesting segue."

"He's not my reporter guy."

"Sorry, your editor guy."

"He's not my editor guy, either."

"I notice you're not telling me I'm wrong about the segue, though. Did something happen?"

"No," she said too quickly. And resisted the urge to rub her lips.

David studied her and nodded. "Did you want it to?"

"Not with him working at the *Gazette,* no."

"Ah."

"Don't say 'ah' like that."

"How about hmm?"

"David," she said warningly.

He gave an innocent smile and leaned back in his chair. "Liz and the kids are great. You should come over. Tash is talking up a storm and you can actually understand some of it. And Emma's crawling."

So different. She remembered the years he'd been resolutely solo, unable to allow himself to deal with the emotional demands of a relationship. Somehow, though, he'd managed to get past it. "You really love it, don't you? Having a family."

"Yeah, I do. I didn't think I would. Didn't think I could, really, not with what happened to us."

"Did you and Liz—" she hesitated "—did you connect? Like us? I don't mean—"

"I know what you mean," he said. "I always figured it was just a twin thing, the way we always kind of know what the other one is thinking. But when I met Liz it was there, from the very beginning. Scared the hell out of me," he added. "Is that what's going on with this guy?"

Jillian sighed. "I can't even think about it, not with him working for the *Gazette.*"

"You know the *Gazette* hasn't been responsible for the worst of it. They wrote some stories—"

"Without ever interviewing Robbie or anyone at the Children's Connection."

"Granted, but they at least came back to the staff at the clinic for the later stories. It's not the *Gazette* that's the problem, it's the tabloids."

"And, gee, where did they get the story?"

"You're smart enough to know you can't hold them accountable for that, Jilly. That's not what's putting you off about this guy."

Jillian glowered. David just gave her a sunny smile and waited. She folded her arms. "He makes me uncomfortable," she said finally.

David's smile widened. "That's usually a good sign. You're too smart to want comfortable."

"That's exactly what I want," she countered. "Big drama plays great on the movie screen but it's dysfunctional as hell in real life. That's not what adult relationships are supposed to be about."

"Any adult relationship is going to have conflict. It's how you deal with it that matters. And comfort is good but you've also got to have differences. You've got to have the edge. That's the spice, that's what makes things interesting."

"Yeah, well, I'm not sure I need interesting right now, not while things are a mess at the clinic and Robbie's gone."

"And when Robbie's back, what's the excuse going to be then?" he asked gently. "You can't keep running away any more than Robbie can. I tried with Liz, in the beginning. I ran like hell. And then one day I decided I wasn't going to let what happened to us as kids rule the rest of my life. And you can't, either."

She finished her tea and rose. "I know, but it's not something I'm ready to deal with now." Her voice was brisk.

"I take it that's my cue to go?" he asked.

"I think your family might be happy to see you for dinner," she told him. They took the shortcut through the house and on the front porch she kissed his cheek. "Thanks for coming by and thanks for caring about me," she said. "It'll be all right. Trust me, I know about these things. I'm a social worker."

"That means you're really good at taking care of other people. What about taking care of you?"

"It's on my list of things to do," she said. Behind her, the phone rang. "Oops, gotta get that."

"Did you pay someone to call?" David asked.

Jillian laughed. "I'll never tell." Shutting the door, she went back to pick up the receiver. "Hello?"

There was no reply. All she heard was the fuzz of an empty line and an occasional swishing sound that might have been trucks and cars driving by.

"Hello?" she repeated. "Is anyone there?"

Silence, but the person didn't hang up. The seconds ticked by and Jillian's heart began to thump harder. "Robbie?" she whispered. "Is that you?"

With a click, the line disconnected.

Chapter Six

There were a lot of things Gil appreciated about living downtown—good restaurants, good music, a ten-minute commute—but none of them meant quite as much as his morning runs along the river.

If anyone asked him, he'd say he was a solitary guy. It was just that he had a job and a life that meant he spent a lot of time hanging out with people and socializing. He went clubbing, hit receptions and parties, took women out—and took them to bed.

But few of those women could say they really knew him. When the laughter died away, few of his friends knew what he was about. That was all right with Gil. Maybe it was growing up with his father and much-older brothers in a household of exclusively men, maybe it was growing up the son of a logger. Toughness and self-sufficiency had always been prized in his house, qualities he'd held on to.

Even when he'd flown in the face of his father's wishes and gone into journalism.

"Get a real job where you work," Tom Reynolds had scoffed, "not one where you kiss off all the time and stick your nose where it doesn't belong." There was no sense wasting a college degree on a job that would never pay, he'd maintained. "Forget this Woodward and Bernstein jazz. You want to go, get an engineering degree, something that'll make you a living. Don't expect me to pay for it, though."

By then, Gil had already known not to expect anything, at all. That was all right, he was happier doing it himself—and showing the old man while he was at it. So he worked his way up through the ranks from intern to reporter to editor, fighting for that next scoop, developing sources, honing his instincts until at thirty-eight he was city editor of the top newspaper in Portland. Being a newspaperman didn't make him soft; he proved that to himself every day. On the contrary, to do the job right, he had to be tough, hardworking and keep his feelings out of it.

Of course, cooking up a profile to give him an excuse to be around Jillian Logan wasn't exactly keeping his feelings out of it. It was a way to give Gleason what he wanted without doing irresponsible coverage, though, so it was nearly justifiable.

Nearly.

Except that it wasn't Gleason or the *Gazette* he thought of as he headed back to his condo. It was Jillian, her mouth, her taste, the feel of her hot against him. And if she thought she'd discouraged him at lunch, she was very much mistaken. After that kiss at the wedding, there was no putting the genie back in the bottle. There was something between them and he wasn't going to walk away until they were done with it.

And if his job profile made Russ happy by putting the Logans back on the front page, so much the better.

"Morning, Jillian."

"Hi, Sue." Jillian crossed the lobby of the Children's Connection, smiling at receptionist Sue Martinelli. "How was your weekend?"

"Great. Ron and I went to Astoria. How about yours?"

"Not nearly long enough," Jillian replied.

Sue snorted. "Are they ever?"

Not this time around, Jillian thought as she walked into her office, not when she had to face Gil Reynolds first thing in the morning. Then again, no one had ever gotten back to her about a time. For all she knew, Gil wasn't showing up today. Maybe, she thought with a hope she recognized immediately as vain, he wasn't showing up at all.

Fat chance.

As if to underscore the point, her phone rang. The display showed Sue's number. For an instant, Jillian considered not answering, but ducking out wasn't her style. Sighing, she picked up the reciever. "Hi, Sue. What's up?"

"There's someone out here to see you. A Gil Reynolds from the *Gazette?*"

And that quickly, Jillian's heart rate doubled. Ridiculous, she lectured herself as she rose. She was a professional. She was perfectly capable of keeping the situation under control. Gil was here to do a job and so was she—for the Children's Connection. As long as she concentrated on that, everything would stay on an even keel.

And then she walked out the door into the reception area and nothing was even, at all.

Least of all, her pulse.

Gil rose. Jillian had worn low heels with her tailored taupe trouser suit. It left her looking up at him, which was a mistake because it had her remembering that moment in the parking lot at Lisa's wedding.

That moment her mouth had touched his.

"I see you made it," she said.

"Bright and early," he agreed, picking up his computer bag.

"You come prepared."

"I figure I'm not always going to be able to follow along with you."

He wore an olive-colored suit and a black-and-gold patterned tie. Polished and professional, a step above the khakis and twill shirts that seemed to be the uniform for Portland professionals. A sheaf of his dark hair had flopped down over his forehead as though he'd walked out of his house while it was still wet.

"With the computer, I can work during the downtime," he continued and paused. "As opposed to the uptime?"

Jillian blinked at him.

"Like now? Why don't we get started?" he prompted.

She'd been staring, she realized. "Right. Of course. This way." She turned briskly, before the flush could spread up over her cheeks. But not before she caught a flash of his grin.

He followed her through the door from the carpeted lobby to the bright hallways of the heart of the Children's Connection.

"Looks like a medical clinic," Gil observed, craning his neck to see around him.

"It is a medical clinic, at least, in part. IVF is a medical procedure. If you turn at the end of that hall, you hit the walkway that takes you over to Portland General. That's where you'll find the cafeteria and break room and the birthing rooms our nurses use. My office is down here," she added, turning the opposite way.

"Ever get called in to play catch during a delivery when they're shorthanded?"

When she turned to stare at him in the doorway of her office, he just grinned.

Jillian shook her head and walked in to sit at her desk. Calm authority, she thought. The thing to do was keep control of the situation. Hard to do, though, when he made himself comfortable in one of her chairs, sitting back, crossing his legs. How could one person fill a room? she wondered.

Jillian crossed her own legs, resisting the urge to fold her arms. "I can certainly give you a tour of the clinic. What else do you want from me?"

His smile widened. "What is this, a trick question?"

She scowled. "Look, the only reason you're here is because LJ, for reasons best known to himself, thinks it's a good idea. I told him I'd tolerate you but I expect you to act like a professional."

"I'll do my best," Gil said obediently. It didn't wipe the smile away, though. "To answer your question, what I want is to watch as you go through your week. I want you to talk to me about what you do, how you do it and why it's important and satisfying to you."

He wanted to get into her head, she realized uneasily. And for all that she could understand why he might need that, part of her cringed at the thought.

"At some point, I'll want to interview you," he said, confirming her fears.

"Later," she said automatically.

"That's fine. We've got a photographer lined up for Thursday morning, if that works. In the meantime, I'll just sit in the background for your meetings and such."

"You can't sit in on my meetings," she objected. "Not most of them. They're client sessions. It's confidential."

"Even if they agree to it?"

"I wouldn't let them. Having another person in the room violates confidentiality. More important, it changes the dynamic. It's not healthy for the clients and it certainly won't let me do my job effectively."

There it was again, Gil thought, that flash of

protectiveness, the same one she'd shown toward Lisa. It was part of her being, he realized. She would always leap to defend those she felt needed it, no matter what the cost to her.

"I can see why you wouldn't want me in the sessions but I think the article would be incomplete if I don't talk about specifics. What if I interview them afterward? Anonymously," he hastened to add.

"We're still putting them on the spot. I'm sorry. It was a nice idea but this isn't going to work."

He'd been in the business too long to let that scare him off. "According to your PR manager, it will."

"LJ doesn't know my work as well as he does the rest of the clinic," Jillian said.

"Call him," Gil suggested.

"I will," she returned, dialing LJ's cell-phone number even as she spoke. When Gil didn't move, she gave him a pointed stare. "Do you mind?"

Grinning, he stepped out into the hall.

It didn't matter, though, because the line rolled over into voice mail. "This is LJ Logan. On Monday, I'll be flying to New York so I'll be out of contact—" Gritting her teeth, Jillian hung up.

Gil poked his head in the door. "So what did you find out?"

"LJ's not around. He's flying back to New York this morning." Leaving her to deal with things on her own.

"That's all right." Gil sat back down. "Why don't we do this? You ask your clients—the ones you think would be appropriate—if they'd mind talking to me after the sessions. I won't use their real names or any specifics. I just want to give readers a feel for the human face of what you do. It'll be a way to help others, maybe get through to people who are sitting around out there with the same problems, not knowing how to deal with them. What do you say?"

He was pushing her buttons, she was sure of it, but when he put it that way, it was hard to say no. "You'd have to guarantee anonymity."

"They can talk to me from behind a partition if you want," he offered. "Of course, that wouldn't show me what you do in your sessions."

She stared at him like he was a loon. "We talk," she said.

"About what?"

"Whatever the client's issues are. Couples dealing with infertility or adoption, egg donors, a single mother coping with raising a child, a child meeting its prospective parents for the first time. Whatever's necessary."

"Sounds like a grab bag."

"It is. It keeps life interesting. Every day is different."

He raised his eyebrows. "So you like variety? You strike me as someone who likes things organized."

"Is that a nice way of saying I'm anal?" she asked tartly.

His lips twitched. "I think you're looking for hidden meanings, Doc."

"Looking for hidden meanings is my job."

"I'll keep that in mind." Casually, he pulled a compact recorder out of his pocket and set it on the coffee table beside him. "Maybe what we should do is run a mock session. You can show me what it's like, just so I get the experience." His eyes gleamed. "I guess, first, you'd close the door for privacy."

Sudden nerves washed through her. "I don't think we need to be that accurate."

"Sure we do. It'll give me the true feeling." He rose and shut the door.

Instantly, the room shrank. Suddenly, Jillian regretted the warm lighting, the soft furnishings, the homey, intimate air of the space, because with just her and Gil Reynolds in it, it felt too intimate altogether.

He eased down in the chair and gave an impudent smile. "Now you sit in the doctor's chair. Come on," he pressed. "I want to do it right."

"You're making a joke of this," she said.

"Oh, no." He watched her move to her chair by the window.

She'd bought it because it was low and comfortable, because the arrangement of seats helped establish intimacy with her clients. The last thing she wanted was to establish intimacy with Gil Reynolds.

There was something unsettling about his steady gaze. She took a breath, resisting the urge to look away. "Are you happy now?"

"Not yet. But I'm getting there. So say I walked in and said I wanted to adopt. What would you tell me?"

That he'd have to go to the clinic's other social worker because there was no way she could keep a professional distance. "I'd ask you why."

"Why what?"

"Why you wanted to raise a child alone. Single parenthood is a challenging path. Rewarding, but challenging, no matter whether you're a woman or a man. Why not wait and do it the old-fashioned way?"

His gaze was very steady on hers. "Maybe I haven't found the right woman yet."

"Not through lack of trying, I imagine."

"That was harsh."

"Accurate, though, I suspect. Anyway, why the rush? You're a man, you don't have a biological clock to worry about."

"Sure I do." He grinned. "I want to have a kid while I'm still young enough to teach him to play football when he hits junior high."

"And you want a kid?"

"Don't most people?"

"No," she said slowly, "they don't." And she had firsthand knowledge of it.

"Little kids can be right-on. Better than their parents, a lot of times."

"Have you ever spent time around one?"

"My brothers' kids. I've even changed diapers."

"Brave man."

"You'd be more impressed if you'd seen the diapers." He tapped his fingers on his chair arm. "Anyway, aren't you supposed to be asking me about my childhood and stuff?"

"Do you want me to ask you about your childhood?" Jillian asked calmly.

He shrugged. "Don't you usually?"

"In sessions, I typically focus on the client's reason for being here. But since you've introduced the topic, it must have meaning for you. Tell me about your childhood."

He cocked one leg up on the other knee and laced his fingers behind his head. "Well, let's see. I was raised by wolves down in Springfield. When I was old enough, I ran off to join the circus. Tightrope walker," he elaborated.

Springfield, the resolutely blue-collar enclave across the Willamette from the college town of Eugene. Interesting, Jillian thought. She wondered what he'd say if she informed him that his joke told her a great deal about him. "Raised by wolves? The animal kind or the human kind?"

Something flickered in his eyes. "The human kind. My father and my three brothers. Real wolves might have done a better job."

Only years of training kept her from reacting. "Where was your mother?" she asked.

"Dead. She had a massive stroke when I was five. At the grocery store. She was picking up a bottle of bleach and boom, she was down." His smile held no humor. "To this day, I can't stand the smell of Clorox."

"I'm sorry." The words were out before she knew she was going to say them.

"Thanks," he said slowly. And suddenly, their eye contact turned into something more, a tangible connection between them. The seconds stretched out like warm taffy. Jillian had the bizarre impulse to reach out and cover his hand with hers, as though he were next to her rather than across the room.

As though she had a right to.

Abruptly, Gil shook his head and gave a laugh. "Anyway, that was when I joined the circus."

"That's an interesting choice. A different city every night. The perfect excuse for not making a commitment. And your choice of arts—a tight-rope walker. Risk, uncertainty, adrenaline rush."

He shifted a bit. "It was a joke, Doc."

"No." She shook her head. "I don't think it was, entirely."

"What makes you say that?"

"I can hear it in your voice." And the thought of that little boy so many years before tugged on her heart.

The man that the little boy had become sat up in his chair, suddenly tense. She'd seen it before in patients when they'd accidentally revealed more than they'd intended.

"Yeah, well, okay, so I guess that takes care of the sessions," he said, an odd tone to his voice. "How about that tour?"

Jillian hesitated. He wasn't a client. Counseling wasn't why he was here, she reminded herself and rose. "All right."

Fluorescent lights. Walls with pale, mottled mauve wallpaper, gleaming linoleum on the floor. Outside of Jillian's space, the Children's Connection offices were mercifully bright and clinical, washing away that strange moment. Gil shook his head at himself, even as he took notes on the layout.

The fake session thing had started as a lark, a way to yank her chain. He hadn't a clue what had prompted him to actually tell her something real. He wanted to take her to bed, sure, even get to see her for a time. He'd never intended to let her in, though.

He was a man who prided himself on keeping people at arm's length. That was what he'd grown up with. That was what journalists were taught, especially when dealing with subjects. He hadn't a clue what had prompted him to start babbling about stuff long past. Maybe it was her office, a space that felt more like a sitting room than a clinic. Maybe it was that he'd gotten too involved in the role-playing. Maybe it was that way she had of looking at him as though she were listening to him with every fiber of her being, creating that humming link between them like some kind of a tractor beam.

Jillian Logan was good at what she did. Very, very good.

"These are the examining rooms," she said now, waving a hand down the hall.

"What's down there?" He pointed to another door.

She gave him an opaque glance. "The day care center."

The source of all the controversy. "I suppose I should at least see it," he said.

When they neared it, they could hear the laughter of children over the sounds of the SpongeBob SquarePants theme, unless he was much mistaken. The door opened and a brunette stepped out. "Hi, Jillian."

"Hi."

"Who's your friend?"

Jillian hesitated. "He's doing a tour of the clinic."

Gil stepped forward. "Gil Reynolds of the *Portland Gazette*. I'm here shadowing Jillian for a profile."

The woman paled suddenly, her hand in his tensed. He felt more than saw Jillian's sigh.

"Gil, I'd like you to meet Nancy Logan." Jillian paused. "Robbie Logan's wife."

Hell.

The move to introduce himself had been automatic. He'd been a journalist long enough that he knew you could never tell who you might need for a source. Now he knew why Jillian had avoided identifying him, though. Nancy Logan's hand was suddenly damp in his and icy cold, but no cooler than her eyes.

Gil could have thought of a few thousand other things he'd rather do than meet her—hike Mount Hood in bare feet, say, or scrub the Hawthorne Bridge with a toothbrush. It was one thing to okay a story on Robbie Logan; it was another thing to face the man's wife.

Her face held lines of strain; her clothing drooped a little as though she'd recently lost weight. We didn't set out to hurt anyone, he wanted to tell her. We didn't mean to catch you in the cross fire. "Nice to meet you," was all he could say.

Nancy merely nodded. "You'll excuse me."

And that quickly she was gone. Jillian waited only a moment before hurrying after her.

And Gil stood there, feeling like a complete creep.

Jillian burst into the ladies' room after Nancy, who was nowhere in sight. From one of the stalls emanated the sounds of someone being violently ill.

"Nance, is that you?" Jillian asked, wetting a handful of paper towels.

She took the muffled sound of misery as assent and stepped into the neighboring stall to hand the towels under the barrier. Nancy's hand clutched at them. Wanting to give her privacy, Jillian stepped outside to get a cup of water from the cooler. Back in the bathroom, she merely waited, handing the water over when the sounds ceased.

"Thanks." The door to the stall opened and Nancy stepped out, smiling weakly. "Sorry about the disgusting noises."

"No, I'm the one who's sorry. I should have told you Gil was going to be here so you didn't get blindsided. I didn't mean to upset you."

"It wasn't Gil," Nancy said. "I was already feeling queasy."

"Do you have some kind of twenty-four-hour bug?" Jillian watched as Nancy reached in her pocket and pulled out a toothbrush and travel-sized toothpaste. She raised her eyebrows. "Or is it more like a nine-month bug?"

And Nancy's face crumpled.

"Hey," Jillian said. She led Nancy around the corner to the lounge area and sat her on the couch. "Don't cry, Nancy. You should be excited. You're going to be a mom. This is great news."

"No it's not." Nancy blinked and a tear rolled down her cheek. "I'm pregnant and Robbie's gone. He's gone and I don't have a clue where he is. He could be hurt, he could be falling apart. Anything could be happening to him and *I can't help.*" She lowered her face to her hands.

Jillian rubbed her back as she wept. "Nancy, you're not in this alone. We're all here with you, everyone in the family. We all want him home. Robbie will be back."

Nancy sat upright. "When?" she demanded. "He's been gone five weeks and the only thing I've heard from him is one lousy letter. He won't answer his cell phone. He doesn't even know about the baby. And what am I going to do when his probation officer calls?" Her words dissolved into fresh sobs. "I need him back, Jillian."

"I know you do, honey," Jillian murmured, sympathy washing through her as she felt Nancy shake. She herself was upset, the family was upset, but it couldn't hold a candle to what Nancy was feeling, especially now. They had to find Robbie and bring him home before he found himself in worse trouble, that was all there was to it. But unless he was ready to return, it wouldn't do any good at all.

Oh, it was such a mess, Jillian thought in frustration. Damn Gil's paper, anyway.

Gil's paper.

Newspapers could be used to build things up as well as tear them down. If she worked with Gil, really worked with him, maybe she had the power to do more than help the Children's Connection. Maybe she could help Robbie.

And if she had to cultivate Gil Reynolds to do that, she'd do it.

Nancy's storm of weeping finally abated and she raised her head from Jillian's shoulder.

"I guess that was long overdue," Jillian said. "Feel better?"

"A little." She gave a watery smile.

"Good. You know all my numbers. Anytime you need to talk, I'm here. And Nancy, about the baby—" she hesitated "—it's your decision and your news but you should really think hard about telling the family. It's good news we can all use but there's something else more important— they can't help you unless they know. You don't have to do this alone. We're Logans, all of us, and family's there for family. Trust that because it's real."

Nancy looked at her for a long moment and then nodded. "You're right."

"You're going to make my parents very happy," Jillian told her. "The next generation is what family's all about." She leaned in conspiratorially. "And think, in just a couple of weeks you'll get to raid Jenny's closet for all of her maternity clothes."

The day flew by, or maybe it was because Gil found himself fascinated by watching Jillian. He'd always had a knack for getting people to open up to him. It was one of his best skills as a reporter.

Jillian, though, made him look like an amateur. She had a way of creating a circle between her and her clients that made them comfortable with her. It was just like the way he'd found himself drawn in with their little mock session. One moment, he'd been joking around; the next, he'd found himself telling her things that some of his closest friends didn't even know. He still wasn't quite sure how it had happened.

He watched the parade of clients walk into her office full of trepidation and come out relaxed, relieved, bearing signs of upset, perhaps, but better off for it.

And she went through the hours and session

after session without flagging. Her focus was absolute, her attention to her clients complete. Finally, though, the day was done.

"Don't you ever get burned out by the end of the day?" he asked her. "I think if I were you I'd run screaming from anyone who wanted to talk with me, even if they were my best friend."

"You mean compassion fatigue?"

"There's a term for it?"

She gave him a pitying smile. "We social workers have a term for everything. And it's a very real risk."

"So how do you deal with it?"

She shrugged. "Spend time in a totally different environment. Outdoors. A lot of people use exercise or even meditation."

"I didn't mean how do social workers deal with it," he corrected, "I meant how do you?"

And that quickly, she closed up. He could see it in her eyes, in the set of her shoulders and the frustration hit. He'd done dozens of hostile interviews over the years and still come away with information. He tried everything he knew on Jillian Logan and she just shut him out. She might have excelled at listening but the minute he asked her a question about herself, even something as innocuous as where she went to school, she tensed, speaking so slowly it felt as if she was weighing each and every syllable.

Or she didn't answer at all.

"You know, this isn't going to be much of a profile if you won't talk to me," he said.

"I thought it was supposed to be about the job, not me. You're finding out what you need to know about that, aren't you?"

"It won't come together unless we see it all through your eyes. We need to understand your commitment, your rewards. People want to find out how it fits into their world, whether it's something they could do, too. And don't tell me anybody can do anything they want," he preempted her.

"I wouldn't dream of it. We've all got our limitations. That being said, many things are like yoga—it's not a matter of doing the pose perfectly but trying for your best position."

"And in a career like yours, that's a crock. You can't do it halfway. People need a social worker who's doing more than their best pose. They deserve someone like you."

Amusement flickered in her eyes. "A compliment? I thought journalists weren't supposed to get involved with the subject."

"That's kind of a moot point with us already, isn't it?"

"An interesting question but I think we can discuss it tomorrow." She dug in her desk drawer for her purse. "It's time to go home."

"When do I get my interview?"

"Later," she said, echoing her response from the morning.

Outside, the afternoon was mild, the sky dotted with clouds. "I'm parked over here," Gil said. "How about you?"

"You drove? Where do you live?"

"See the corner of that building?" he asked.

She frowned. "Where?"

He leaned in close to point over her shoulder to the condo building, renovated from an old brick-and-iron factory building.

"That close? You could have walked here."

"I suppose. Where do you live?"

"Is this the start of the interview?" she asked in amusement.

"Is later finally now?"

"No. I have to get home."

"Where's home?"

"You are persistent, aren't you?"

"First thing you learn in journalism school—if the subject doesn't answer the question, ask it another way. And I'm going to keep asking, Jillian. That's one thing you should know about me. I don't give up."

He wasn't talking about the interview, she realized. Something fluttered inside her. She needed to do it, for Robbie. And maybe, just maybe, for her. She moistened her lips. "I live in Ladd's Addition."

"Nice. I guess you can't walk from there." He looked her up and down. "You don't look much like a bicycle commuter."

"I'm not sure whether I should take offense at that."

He grinned. "Hardly. Bus or car?"

"I take the bus. Plenty of people do."

"I can give you a ride, then."

She gave him a long, measuring look. A ride home with him wouldn't be relaxing and it wasn't a place she was ready to go with him just then. "Remember how you were just asking me how I deal with compassion fatigue?" she asked. "Part of it is taking the bus. I can be on it with all those other people but nobody knows me, nobody talks to me. I can just sit there and let the day bleed away."

"You can let the day bleed away with a glass of wine and a shoulder massage, too," he commented.

"I like my space," she said.

"And why is that, Doc? You want to talk some more about that?"

She resisted a smile. "Our session's over for today," she told him.

Chapter Seven

"I walked," Gil said as he stepped into Jillian's office the next morning.

She jumped, he saw in satisfaction. Her expression, when she looked at him, was calm and composed. But he saw the little flicker of uneasiness in her eyes.

Good. He was glad he made her uneasy. It meant he was getting to her. Even if it was like picking away at a brick wall with his fingernails, he was starting to pry loose a few flakes. Make that chunks.

He was enjoying this.

"You walked?"

"To get here. I walked this morning." He felt expansive, energized as he set down his laptop case.

Her lips twitched. "Let me duck in back and get you a medal."

He could think of a few things he'd rather have than that, but he figured she probably wouldn't want to hear it. "So what's on the docket for today?" he asked instead.

"The rest of a little boy's life, I hope."

"The rest of a little boy's life?"

She gave him a serene smile. "First, I need to do e-mail and paperwork and update my files. I told you not to show up until ten-thirty."

"I figured I could sit here and absorb the atmosphere, maybe talk to a few of the other folks in the clinic about you." And have a chance to watch her while she worked. "So what about the little boy?"

"I'll tell you on the way to getting him."

His name was Pedro and he was seven. He'd lost his mother at three, leaving him with memories that were just impressions of warmth and safety; his father had disappeared before Pedro had ever been born. For a while, the boy had lived with his mother's younger sister but Tia Essie had kids of her own. More to the point, she had a husband who hit the bottle on a regular basis. And then hit Pedro.

Even before Pedro had gotten into his first foster home at five, he'd learned that the world was a dangerous place for a child. And an even more dangerous place for hope.

By the time Jillian had begun working with him as part of the agreement the Children's Connection had with the state, Pedro had acquired an expressionless mask for the world, the same kind that long-term prisoners acquired. She could see the real boy looking out from behind it, though, like some little lost wild thing hidden in a copse.

She remembered what it had been like.

So she'd spent hours with him, finding him a good foster home, always working to break through. And she'd consulted with Lois, trying to find the key, trying to decide which adoptive parents would be the right ones for him. After that, it had been the slow, gradual process of introducing him to Kathy and Dan Collins, letting him get to know them. Trust? That was going to be an even longer process.

"It's a good place for you," Jillian said to Pedro now as they drove through the Portland streets to the neat southeast neighborhood where Kathy and Dan lived. "You'll have your own room. You've seen the pictures."

"Yeah."

"It's nice. You like Kathy and Dan."

"I guess." The words were elaborately disinterested but there was an undercurrent of tension.

The kid had to be crazy with nerves; at least, Gil would be in his spot. Gil glanced back to where Pedro sat buckled into his seat. "You like baseball, huh?" he asked, studying the kid's ball cap.

Pedro looked out the window. "I guess," he said tonelessly.

"Who's your favorite player? Ichiro?"

Pedro flicked a disdainful glance at him. "Ichiro hits like a girl. I like Adrian Beltré."

"Ichiro won a batting title and a world record hitting like a girl," Gil observed mildly.

"Beltré's my man. He's a slugger."

Confident, now, Gil noticed. So he continued to push. "You play, yourself? Little League?"

Pedro watched the houses pass by. "Yeah."

"What was your team?"

"The Red Sox."

"What position do you play?"

"Third base," Pedro said.

"The hot corner."

Pedro dipped his head. "Kind of."

It surprised Gil. Most kids liked first base, where all the action was. "Are you good at it?"

A reluctant grin tugged at the corners of the kid's mouth. "Yeah," he said. "I'm good."

The car slowed and they pulled to a stop in

front of a tidy yellow ranch house that was straight out of the fifties, with bricked-in planters and a neat flagstone walk. A couple stepped outside onto the front porch, beaming and nervous, the woman in a flowered shirt and walking shorts, the man in jeans and a T-shirt.

And a baseball cap.

"I guess we're here, buddy," Gil said. "You ready for it?"

Pedro was slow getting out of the car, careful walking up the front path, looking all around him as though determined not to miss a detail. When he reached Kathy and Dan, he gave a small smile.

"Hey," Dan said.

"Hi," Pedro returned. They didn't hug or touch, Gil noticed. The kid looked stiff enough that if you bent him, he'd break.

"Come on in," Kathy invited, some of the tension leaking over to her.

Pedro brought the same watchful, serious attention to the inside of the house, walking through it as though he were somewhere he wasn't allowed to be, as though he expected to be booted out any minute. It was interesting. Gil had expected a boy with the kind of background Jillian had described to be excited about a real home. Maybe life had taught him that a smart guy didn't bank on anything.

Gil had to hand it to the couple, they let the kid

wander, let him take his time looking around. No matter that it obviously disappointed them and cost them. Even when Kathy showed Pedro his room with a kind of nervous pride at the fresh paint and new dresser, the reaction was guarded. The conversation grew more and more constrained, even with Jillian doing her best to guide it. They walked out to the kitchen.

And then Gil saw it by the door to the garage: a glove and bat tossed up against the wall. He knew the exact moment Pedro realized it was there. The kid came to absolute attention. For the first time, that mask of calm and distance slipped.

He walked to it, staring down.

"Dan plays city league softball," Kathy said, picking up the bat.

Something flickered in Pedro's eyes. "Softball?"

Dan nodded. "Third base."

"The hot corner," Pedro said.

Dan grinned. "Maybe not when I play it. It's a little more lukewarm. Hey, you want to see the backyard?"

Pedro reached the sliding-glass door to the backyard, a sweep of emerald grass. At the far end was chain-link fence with wood slats fed through it to create a solid-appearing barrier. Pedro shot an inquiring glance at Kathy, who nodded, and he stepped outside.

He walked across the grass, more relaxed now. There was a pole stuck in the ground with a ball on ropes, one of those gizmos for hitting practice that let you wind the rope up so that the ball came flying back around like a pitch. Pedro walked over to unwind the ball and rope from around the pole and give it a whirl.

"I use it to practice my swing," Dan said. "If you want, we could go get the bat and hit a few. Or there's a batting cage I know of."

Pedro was starting to move more freely now, crossing the grass to the fence. And then he put his eye to the gaps between the slats and saw what Gil could already see over the top—the elementary school playground beyond, complete with basketball hoops, swings, tetherball poles…

And a baseball diamond where a group of kids were playing a hotly contested game of pickup baseball.

For just an instant Pedro smiled, really smiled. And it was brilliant. "They play baseball there?" he said.

Dan nodded, the smile contagious. "Little League, during the season. That's just a bunch of the neighborhood kids out there playing. Jeremy next door, some of the other kids on the street. Why, do you play?"

"Oh, yeah," Pedro breathed. "Oh, yeah."

"What position?"

Pedro's eyes flicked to Gil. "The hot corner." The kid's lips twitched. Just a flicker, but suddenly Gil knew it was going to be all right.

Jillian's face was just luminous.

He'd never thought much about family. Sure, he had his, but they'd been a challenge as much as a support. And he'd been honest with Jillian when he'd told her that he figured on probably having kids someday, but he'd never figured on someday being anytime in the immediate future.

Watching Dan and Pedro as they took turns using the ball on the rope to practice their swings, though, he was beginning to think that someday might just be sooner rather than later, after all.

"You want to know why I do it?" Jillian asked as they drove away from dropping Pedro back at his foster home. "For days like this."

She felt as if she was floating above the ground. She felt ten feet tall, giddy. Days like this made it all worthwhile—the hours, the stress, the discouraging periods, the times she left work feeling sucked dry. At a moment like this, life was beautiful. At a moment like this, she could kiss someone.

She glanced over at Gil, beside her.

He'd helped make it work, she realized. Maybe he was only getting them where they would have eventually gone anyway, but he'd helped Dan and Kathy connect. He'd known instinctively the right strings to pull. Maybe it was just the people skills of a journalist, the ability to set people at ease.

And maybe it was just him.

They sat at an intersection, waiting for a Burlington Northern switch engine to move out of the way. Caution: Remote-Controlled Engine, warned a sign.

"There's something I always find deeply disturbing about that idea," Gil commented.

"I know what you mean. A remote-controlled model airplane is one thing. I don't think anything as big as a diesel engine ought to run on its own."

He whistled. "You know this is probably a first," he said.

"What?"

"You've agreed with me on something."

"There must be a blue moon this month."

"I think you're going sweet on me," he said, enjoying it when she blushed. This wasn't the cool, self-contained woman he'd become accustomed to. This wasn't the hostile opponent. There was a light, happy, almost incandescent air about her. He wanted to hold on to this moment, keep that young, free look in her eyes.

"How about lunch?" he suggested.

"Lunch?"

"Sure. I'll even buy. I know a place a couple of blocks away that we can go. I think you'll like it."

"Well…"

"You told me yourself that you didn't have any meetings until afternoon. Come on. You've got to eat."

"I've got work," she objected.

"Forget work. For right now, ride the buzz. You're allowed. You just won the social worker's version of the World Series. We need to celebrate."

That earned him a grin. "Okay, you're on."

The Hedge House was tucked away in an old clapboard house in the southeast part of the city. The food was good pub food, the beer worth a return visit. And if the waitstaff was occasionally—frequently— irreverent, it was always in a good way.

"Aren't we a little far from your stomping grounds?" she asked as he steered her to the back deck.

"I applied for a VISA," he told her. They sat at one of the wooden picnic tables and soaked in the warm afternoon. "I was here one time with a buddy and the waiter came rolling by on a skateboard."

She raised her eyebrows. "A skateboard?"

"I swear. Now, really, you have to come back to a place like that. Besides, I like the deck. We don't get enough summer. I try to take advantage of it."

"You wouldn't appreciate it nearly as much if

you lived somewhere where it was nice all the time. It would just get boring."

"I don't know, when I see Floridians on TV, they don't usually look bored."

"They're acting for the camera. Anyway, you're enough of a tough guy that a little Portland mist's not going to frighten you off."

His lips twitched as their waiter brought them drinks. "Are you psychoanalyzing me?"

"I don't know, should I be? Know thy enemy?"

"I'm not your enemy," he said. "I think you know that by now. Anyway, I assumed you therapists could figure people out at a glance."

"Social workers," she corrected. "And I haven't really studied you yet."

"I'm not so hard to figure out."

"On the contrary. I think you're a lot more complicated than you let on," she countered, leaning forward.

"So you have been studying me."

She appeared endearingly embarrassed. "Well, I can't shut off my brain entirely when I talk to people."

"I bet. Do people shy away from you at parties because they're worried about being psychoanalyzed?"

"I don't go to parties."

"Why not?"

"I see enough people in the course of my day. I like having time to myself after."

"So what do you do with yourself when you're not working?"

She gave him an amused look. "Is this the interview?"

"No. Just simple curiosity."

Wariness flickered in her eyes for the first time. "This and that."

His lips twitched. "This and that, huh?"

A hint of color stained her cheekbones. "How do I know this won't wind up in the paper?"

"'Outside her job, Logan spends her time doing this and that,'" he quoted. "You're right, it is kind of a scoop. What, is it something really scandalous? Do you have a backyard fois gras operation? Do you deal in counterfeit organic tomatoes? Come on, give me something I can make a story out of."

"You're making me sound silly."

"You're being silly. How about this? The whole conversation here is off the record. Just between you and me."

The waiter appeared—sans skateboard—and brought drinks, pausing to take their food order before disappearing.

Gil raised his pint. "Here's to Pedro, a good kid who's about to get his first real break. And here's to you for bringing it to him."

"I had a lot of help. Lois, Kathy and Dan, the foster parents he's been living with, his Social-Services social worker. You," she added.

"Me?"

"You got him talking. What you just saw was one of the trickiest transitions in the process. You helped him loosen up, helped him find something to fasten on to. I thought journalists weren't supposed to get involved. Why did you?" she asked curiously.

"Hey, not so loud or I'll get kicked out of the club," he said.

"That's not an answer. Now who's holding back?"

Gil shrugged. "I don't know. I just figured it couldn't hurt to get him talking. He looked kind of lost, like he was scared to death and trying not to show it."

"He's had a tough life. He's learned that change isn't always good. So thanks."

Gil considered. "So what you're really saying is that you should be buying lunch for me instead of vice versa."

Jillian's lips twitched. "Maybe I should," she said. "Maybe I should."

Chapter Eight

The lunch buzz carried them through the rest of the afternoon, but eventually Jillian went into an end-of-day staff meeting and the doors shut in Gil's face. He tried to bear it with good grace—after all, they had let him sit in on the opening marketing discussion and he got to watch an animated Jillian talk about ways to reach birth mothers, one of the clinic's key groups to help. Eventually, though, the doors closed.

There was nothing more frustrating for a journalist than to be shut out of the action. Okay, so they were talking specifics. Just because he could understand it didn't make it any less annoying to get booted out.

It only took a few minutes of sitting in the break room for him to be certain that the lobby was a better option. He'd asked Jillian about using her office but she'd hesitated just long enough to make it clear she was uneasy at the prospect. It wasn't worth it, not with the fragile bond that was forming between them.

Even if it had meant that he could have spent a happy hour surrounded by her scent while he worked.

Finally, he chose the lobby. Sue, the receptionist was gone, the day nearly over, so he could expect to find both comfortable chairs and quiet.

At least, at first. When the bell sounded on the door, he glanced over to see a young woman walk into the clinic, her long, red hair hanging loose around her shoulders.

"Oh." She stopped before the empty receptionist's desk and looked blankly around at him. "Where is she?"

"I think there's a staff meeting," he said. "Give it about fifteen minutes and someone should be out."

The girl nodded and sat. Tension vibrated off her. She picked up a magazine and leafed through a few pages, then set it back down. Stepped across the room to pick up a different one and set it down, too. Restless, Gil diagnosed, watching her circle around, glancing at the pictures on the walls. Families and children, playing together, living together.

Women in the delivery room, cradling their infants.

Rubbing her stomach, she turned abruptly away and walked to the closed door that led to the back, peering into the frosted window above the doorknob. "What's taking them so long?" she asked, a thread of desperation in her voice.

Not his business, Gil reminded himself, but he couldn't stop watching her. She paced some more, walking to the front door and then turning back. Out of the corner of his eye he saw her touch her face, once, then twice.

And then he realized she was crying.

Oh, hell, he thought, women and tears, his worst nightmare. And yet even though it gave him the willies, even though he knew he shouldn't get involved, he couldn't help himself. "Hey." He kept his voice soft. "What's going on?"

"Where are they?" Impatience, urgency and, under it all, a hint of anxiety.

"They'll be back soon."

"But I can't stay. I have to get back." And she was afraid, deathly afraid, to judge by the way her hands were shaking.

"Wait here. I'll get someone." He spoke before he knew he was going to.

"No. I really don't have a lot of time." She was two steps from bolting, he realized.

"Trust me." In her eyes he saw the fear, the desperation. "They're good people here. Whatever the problem is, they'll help you. Look, give me a couple of minutes to find someone. I'll be right back. Just stay, promise?"

Slowly, her gaze never leaving his, she nodded.

Back in the clinic, the conference-room door was still shut. Gil didn't give a damn. He walked up, gave a sharp rap and opened it. A dozen faces turned to him inquiringly.

"I need Jillian," he said abruptly.

She wasn't pleased. "This is a closed meeting." He could hear the impatience in her voice.

"You've got someone out front you need to talk to."

It could have been his tone or his gaze, but something got through to her. She was up and out the door in a flash. "What is it?" she asked as she passed him at the threshold.

"A young girl, maybe eighteen. She looks pretty upset. I figured you were a good place to start, assuming she hasn't bolted."

She hadn't. She was close—on her feet and pacing near the front door, but she was still there.

He walked up, Jillian in tow. "See, I told you I'd be back," he said to the girl. "She'll help you."

Jillian put out her hand. "I'm Jillian Logan, the social worker at the clinic."

The girl didn't quite manage a smile. "I'm Alison."

"Nice to meet you, Alison. Would you like to go back to my office? It's a more comfortable place to talk."

It was amazing to watch Jillian in action. There was something about the way she focused on people, Gil thought as he followed inside, stopping himself at the little anteroom outside her office. It was as though the people she was trying to help were the only ones who existed for her in that place and time. She listened with her whole body, her whole being.

He suddenly, fiercely found himself wanting her to look at him that way. Not because he was a client but because he was a man.

Her man.

"So what's going on, Alison?" Jillian asked softly.

"I'm pregnant," Alison blurted, and buried her face in her hands. For long moments, she just wept, as though she'd held it all in and now it was safe to let herself feel the fear and anxiety.

Jillian waited her out, knowing what it had cost the girl to come. And feeling stupidly grateful to Gil for figuring it out. It was one thing to talk baseball with Pedro. It was another for him to clearly break with his journalistic training and intercede.

Finally, Alison started talking through her tears. "I'm at the university on scholarship," she said. "I just finished my freshman year."

"What's your major?"

"Education. I want to teach. I've always wanted to teach. It's just that it was after finals and I was at this party. And things went south with my boyfriend back at Christmas, so I haven't been with anyone in forever. I met this really cute guy and we wound up going back to my room, just fooling around. And it was so dumb. I can't believe I did it. But it was just so hot and I don't usually drink and you know what it's like when you're with someone when it's just rocking your world." The words tumbled out. "I just thought this once it'd be okay. I couldn't possibly get pregnant just this once. Except that I did." She began to cry again.

"What do you want to do?"

"I can't tell my parents. They'll be appalled. And we don't have any money, anyway. I can only afford to be here because of scholarships and loans. All that would be over. And I can't raise a baby." Her voice rose in fear. "I'm still a kid, myself. I can't do this. I want kids someday, but now?"

Clearly, the idea terrified her.

"What does the father say?"

She shook her head. "He's premed. Totally freaked out at the idea of a baby. He told me it was my problem." Her voice was bitter.

"You have choices." Jillian's voice was gentle. "You can have the baby and keep it. You can terminate, though we'd have to refer you on that one. Or you could put it up for adoption."

This prompted fresh tears. "But then I'd never know where she was or how she was or who had her."

"That's not necessarily the case. Adoptions are much more open now. A lot of times there's contact between the birth parents and the child—anything from a letter once a year to visits. And you'd screen prospective parents, really find out who they are and whether they're the kind of people you want raising your child. You've got choices, Alison. We can help you with all of them. And you don't have to decide right away."

"I do have to decide. It's already been a month since I was sure. It's just... It's all so overwhelming."

"It's a challenging spot but we're here to help you any way we can. You're not alone anymore. In fact..."

"What?"

"Well, I know someone who was in your shoes. Worse, really. She was living on the streets at the time. Now, she's got a college degree and a career and she just got married. You see? Pregnancy isn't the end, it's just the beginning."

"She got a degree? Really?"

Jillian nodded. "Would it help to talk with her? Not to decide anything, just to talk to someone who's been in your shoes?"

Alison looked at her gratefully. "Do you think she'd do that?"

"I know she would. She just got back from her honeymoon a couple of days ago, but let me call her and see when she could get together with you. In the meantime—" Jillian rose and turned to her desk "—we should get you in to see a doctor to make sure everything is all right. You can take these brochures. One's on prenatal care. The number's there to call for an appointment. And these two give you more information on adoption." Jillian dug into one of her desk drawers and brought out some sample packs of pills. "Here, take these."

"What are they?" Alison turned them to look at the front and the back.

"Vitamins. The baby has a lot of important development going on right now. It's a good idea to follow the vitamin regimen, no matter what you think you might decide. You've got a baby now and you need to care for it properly."

"I'm already taking vitamins," Alison said shyly. "I looked up some information online."

The smile spread over Jillian's face. "You're going to be all right, Alison. One way or another, you'll figure it out. And we're here to help." Jillian handed her a card. "This has all my contact numbers. I'm always on call. If you have questions, if you're upset, if you just need to talk with someone, pick up the phone. I'm here."

Alison clutched the card as if it were a lifeline. "I don't have any money," she said.

"It doesn't matter," Jillian says. "I don't care about that. I care about you."

Alison looked at her for a moment in wonder. "You really mean that, don't you?"

"Depend on it," Jillian said. And breaking one of her rules, she gave the girl a hug. Alison held on fiercely, then released, wiping away more tears. Jillian stood back and studied her, her hands on the girl's shoulders. "Are you going to be okay?"

"Yeah."

"Come on, then."

Jillian walked Alison out through the now-empty offices to the lobby and let her out. It was going to be all right, she thought. They'd help Alison so that she could find her answers.

It was strange, Jillian thought as she stood outside the clinic and watched Alison walk down the sidewalk. The girl was so young, inexperienced, and yet she was comfortable in a world of male and female relationships that Jillian knew nothing of. She could talk casually of things that were mysteries for Jillian.

You know what it's like....

Except that she didn't, Jillian thought. She was fifteen years older than Alison and she hadn't a clue.

Jillian walked back into the clinic. There was no reason to feel inadequate because she was a virgin. It was silly to feel that she was less of a woman. She couldn't help it, though. Somehow, she always felt incomplete, closed down, set apart from the rest of the world.

As she turned down toward her office, she stopped. In the waiting area, Gil sat, laptop on his knees, tapping busily at his keyboard. She'd been out of her mind when she'd decided he wasn't handsome, Jillian thought, staring at that wide, straight mouth, at the dark slash of his eyes. There was more to him than looks, though. In the beginning, she'd thought him clever and funny, generous, if a bit careless. Later, she'd hated him for what he'd done at the paper. Now, she was beginning to wonder if she'd misjudged him in more than looks.

Without warning, he glanced up. The visual contact snapped through her like a physical touch.

For a moment, she didn't move, couldn't. For a moment, she just looked.

"Everything okay?" Gil asked, watching her.

Jillian stepped forward, exaggeratedly aware of her every movement. "I think so. I gave her some information. She mostly needed someone to talk with."

"Pregnant, right?"

"You know I can't tell you that."

"It wasn't hard to figure out." He followed her into her office. "That's why I came and got you."

"You did the right thing." She turned to him, found him closer than she'd realized. "I owe you an apology for snapping at you when you came into the meeting," she said, resisting the urge to step back. "I should have realized you wouldn't have done it if it weren't for good reason."

"Hey, we journalists have a rep for being pushy."

"It made all the difference. She could have walked away; now she's got information, an idea about options. And that's all because of you."

He grinned. "Maybe you should bring me on as your assistant."

"Maybe I should. You surprised me today. No," she corrected herself, "that came out wrong. I just… I guess, I didn't expect you to get involved. I thought journalists were supposed to keep their distance."

He reached out to tuck a strand of hair behind her ear. "Maybe I don't want to keep my distance."

Jillian swallowed. "I'm talking about work."

"I'm not," he said softly.

The breath backed up in her lungs. He was too close, Jillian thought in alarm as he settled his hands on her upper arms. He was too close and there wasn't enough air. "Why me?" she asked, a thread of desperation shivering in her voice.

"Oh, maybe because you're gorgeous." He traced his fingertip down her nose. "Smart." The finger continued along the groove of her upper lip. "Funny." He traced the outline of her lips, leaning closer. "Caring." He curved his fingers around the back of her neck to draw her closer. "And incredibly sexy."

Something began to coil in her, a heat, a tension.

"I can't stop thinking about you," Gil murmured, so close she could feel him form the words. "I dream about you at night. I wake up wanting you."

His eyes on hers never wavered. There were gold flecks around the edges of his pupils, Jillian realized, like little sparks of fire. Helplessly, she stared up at him, her lips parting.

And then his mouth was on hers.

It wasn't like their first kiss. This was no tender exploration, no soft experiment. He took it hard and fast and deep. And as though she'd stepped into a rushing river, she was in over her head, swept away.

Arousal flowed over her, liquid and hot. Always in the past, she'd been able to keep herself separate from the embrace, keep control. Now, control was the last thing she thought of. Heat billowed through her, spiked with desire. It was taste, it was touch, it was texture. In the onslaught of sensation, they all blurred together into one overwhelming mixture that she couldn't possibly resist.

It was like walking through a fun house, each room more impossibly filled with sensations and surprises than the last. Just as she thought she'd discovered all a kiss could bring her, there was more, until she was half gasping, half laughing with it.

And then the hunger took over. Suddenly, just accepting what he gave her wasn't enough. Suddenly, she was impatient for more. And without really even understanding herself, she took.

It was too much; Gil knew from the beginning that it was too much. Too fast, too hard, too desperate. Too urgent. His kiss held all the suppressed wanting of the past days, the days she'd been off-limits, out of reach. But now she was feverish and urgent in his arms and he couldn't stop himself from tasting. He couldn't stop himself from taking. And he couldn't stop himself from needing.

He felt the change in her, like dry tinder gone

to flame. Her mouth was hot and eager and demanding against his. She twisted closer as though she were trying to press their two sets of molecules into one. It drove him nuts, feeling her soft, springy curves, smelling that intoxicating scent that hovered just above her skin. He wanted to touch her, he wanted to know her.

He wanted her naked.

Feverishly, he ran his hands down her back, molding her curves until he could feel himself stirring against her, getting hard.

For an instant, she went absolutely still.

And then Jillian was pulling herself away, dragging her hands through her hair. "I must be out of my mind," she muttered.

Gil was breathing as though he'd just run the hundred-yard dash. All he wanted to do was pull her back to him. But the game was up for now.

And if he had a couple of hours and a lot of cold water, maybe he could convince his body of that.

It would take some convincing, that was for sure. He'd been with a lot of women over the years and no one had ever taken him so far with just a kiss. And now she was pacing away, leaving him standing there.

"Want to tell me what's going on inside that head of yours?" he asked, watching her.

"That I'm too old to be taking stupid chances,

for one. We're in my office. Anyone could have walked in."

"It's after working hours."

"Thank God for small favors," she said. "You—" she pointed at him as he moved toward her "—keep your distance. We're supposed to be acting like professionals."

"Looks like we both fell off the wagon. Maybe we should take it off-line."

"*No.*"

"Oh, come on, Jillian. You're not really going to try to pretend you didn't like it, are you?"

She hesitated. "No, I'm not. But it doesn't matter."

"Doesn't matter? There's something going on here. You don't just ignore that."

Her eyes flashed. "It's not that easy, Gil. Yes, there's chemistry. I don't have to tell you that. But there's still the *Gazette* and my brother and this clinic. And I can't just shrug all that off, not even for whatever it is that's going on here. No matter how good it is." She opened her mouth as if she was going to say more and then shook her head. "Now, it's been a long day and I'm going home."

"Go ahead and go home. And when you come back tomorrow, I'll be waiting." He walked up and brushed a quick kiss over her lips before she realized his intent. "I'm going to keep being here, Jillian. You'd better get used to it."

Chapter Nine

"Want to tell me what we're doing here again?" Gil asked as he and Jillian walked down the street off MLK Boulevard in northeast Portland. Gentrification had spread to many parts of the city; when it hit this part of the northeast, though, it had turned tail and run. Bars covered the windows and graffiti laced the sides of the buildings. The very air felt hard—used. As much as she was currently working to keep her distance from Gil, Jillian was happy to have him around as they walked.

And a sneaky little part of her way down deep was happy to have him around, period.

Which was part of the problem. There was no

point in trying to lie to herself about what had happened in her office the night before. She'd wanted to kiss him. She'd liked it. And she'd wanted more. Despite everything that lay between them, she'd wanted more.

And that was the last thing she could allow herself.

She knew all the measured reasons why not. Family, Robbie, the clinic, the paper. She could tell herself that Gil Reynolds didn't take responsibility for the damage his work at the paper inflicted. She could tell herself that he was so focused on his mission that he didn't admit to himself the toll it took on people's lives.

She couldn't tell herself that he wasn't a good man, though. She couldn't tell herself that he didn't care.

And she couldn't tell herself that she wasn't attracted to him, however much she might have wanted to.

She'd gone home the night before with her thoughts chasing in circles. She'd woken up that morning with no better idea of what to do.

Time, she told herself, but she wasn't at all sure that would help.

"There it is." She pointed ahead. "Advocate Aid. That's why we're here."

"What is it, some Social-Services agency?"

"A nonprofit that provides legal advice to people who can't afford it. I volunteer one Wednesday a month." She glanced at him. "I told you we could skip the shadowing today. This isn't really part of your story."

And God knew she could have used a day to get her thoughts together about him. Currently, they were still firmly scrambled. Not that a day would have given her time to work things out, but it would have been nice to have at least been able to function normally for a few hours. Since the kiss the night before, she'd had a disconcerting tendency to get all breathless every time Gil came within ten feet of her. Which, since he was still supposed to be her shadow, happened fairly often.

"Not part of the story?" Gil responded. "What are you talking about? Of course it is." He opened the swinging glass door that led into the storefront offices of Advocate Aid. "Doing this kind of community work gets to the heart of what social workerdom is all about."

She couldn't help being amused. "Social workerdom?"

"You know what I mean. You volunteer. Most of us just think about it or give it lip service. It says something about you. The reason you do it is the same reason you became a social worker in the first place, I'm guessing."

"I don't do that much," she said uncomfortably. "Lots of people do more."

"Jillian!" An auburn-haired whirlwind came around the corner, a stack of folders in her arms.

"Speaking of which," Jillian said.

The whirlwind resolved itself as Sarajane Gerrity, nerve center, energy supply and beating, bleeding heart of Advocate Aid.

"Who's this," Sarajane demanded, "your bodyguard? I keep telling you the neighborhood isn't that bad." On the desk behind her, a phone began ringing.

Jillian laughed. "No, this is Gil Reynolds from the *Gazette*. He's shadowing me this week for a story. Gil, this is Sarajane Gerrity. She runs the place."

"A reporter, huh?" Sarajane's eyes lit up. "Feel like doing a little pro bono work? I've got a couple of press releases I need written."

Gil shifted uneasily. "I'm supposed to be here covering a story."

"*Short* press releases. I've been meaning to— Excuse me," she said. Balancing the files against one hip, she snatched up the phone. "Advocate Aid, Sarajane. Oh, right, Mrs. Henderson. Yes, he'll be in this afternoon. Give me your number and I'll have him call you back. Great, bye." Snatching up a pen, she scribbled the number on one of her files and hung up the phone. "Anyway,

I've been trying to find time to do them for the last three weeks but—" behind her, the phone began shrilling again. She shrugged "—you see what it's like. Anyway, if you were interested in doing a little volunteer work, it's just the thing." Another line hit on the phone just as the front door buzzed to indicate a walk-in.

"What do you need done?" Gil sighed.

Sarajane grinned. "A release on our new legal director and another on our expanded operating hours."

"New legal director?" Jillian asked. "Anyone I know?"

"Jordan Hall, would you believe it? He's left Morrison and Treherne permanently." She folded the stack of folders up against her chest.

"Jenny's brother? I'd say you have a convert, Sarajane. And what's that on your hand?" she demanded, staring at the winking stone. "That's beautiful. When did you get it?"

Sarajane glowed. "Last weekend."

Jillian held up Sarajane's hand. "It's gorgeous."

"Isn't it?" Sarajane admired the engagement ring herself. "It's a tension-mounted diamond in platinum. Jordan said it reminded him of me." She grinned. "Can't imagine why." She turned back to Gil. "So what did you decide, champ?"

Gil blinked.

"About the press release?"

He gave Jillian a hunted look.

"Don't look at me," she said. "It's your call."

"How long?" he asked Sarajane.

"How should I know? You're the reporter. Maybe two or three hundred words? I don't need it immediately," she assured him. "Friday would do."

"Friday would—" He shook his head. "Give me whatever material you've got."

"Excellent." Sarajane beamed and unearthed it from the stack of folders she held.

"What the… How did you know to have that with you?"

"I believe in being prepared."

"To press gang any innocent person who walks through the door," Jillian clarified.

"Your fiancé didn't by any chance try to get that ring made in titanium instead of platinum, did he?" Gil asked.

Sarajane gave him a merry look. "Maybe. You can ask him while you're interviewing him. He'll be in this afternoon."

"You know, I can't decide if that smile of yours is smug or just satisfied." Gil studied Alan over the top of his pint. They sat in the bar at the Cascade Brewery. Blues played in the background. On the television over the bar, a Mariners batter was working the count against Mussina of the Yankees. "I take it married life version 2.0 is working?"

"So far married life version 2.0 has been great," Alan told him. "This one is going to work for the long haul."

"And you and Lisa are going to stick around Portland for a while?"

"At least until her son is grown."

"Good. I need someone to fleece in poker." Gil took another swallow of his beer.

Alan snorted. "You forget about the Texas part of Texas Hold'em? I grew up playing the game."

"I wondered when you perfected your losing ability."

"Next thing, you're going to start giving me advice on women."

"Until Lisa, you've always needed it. Come on, who tried to warn you about Sherri?"

"Yeah, there was that."

Around them, the pub erupted in cheers as the Mariners batter sent one sailing out of the park for a grand slam.

"Speaking of women, what do you know about Jillian Logan?" Gil asked when things had quieted down again.

"Outside of the fact that she'd hate your guts if she knew what you did at the *Gazette?*"

"I already found out that part."

"Don't say I didn't warn yo—" Alan did a double take. "Found out? Found out how?"

"Personal discussion."

"Personal discussion?"

"*Heated* personal discussion."

Alan closed his eyes for a moment. "Please tell me it was after the wedding."

"A couple of days." Gil shrugged. "I was going to tell her, anyway. She just found out first."

"You were going to tell her, anyway? You get a sudden urge to bare your conscience?"

Gil shrugged. "I wanted to see her again."

"Wait a minute." Alan shook his head like a dog shaking off water. "Okay, here you are, the guy who always has three or four hot women dangling. And here's this woman who you know is going to pick you as the lowest form of human life. And she's the one you go after? You suddenly get hung up on rejection?"

"Thanks for the analysis, Dr. Freud," Gil muttered.

"So what's the fascination?"

Gil moved his glass around on the bar. "I don't know. She's not easy. She takes keeping up with, but that's a good thing. She makes me—"

"What?"

"She makes me want to be better," he said slowly.

Alan gave a long, low whistle.

"What?"

"You might be stuck, my friend," Alan said, and took a swallow of his beer. "And that might be a problem if she's as ticked as you—" He stopped. "Oh, hell, I've got to tell Lisa. This is going to screw everything up."

"What do you mean? Jillian's ticked at me, not her."

"There might be a little question of why Lisa didn't tell her before the wedding."

"Maybe, but I doubt it. She seemed a little more focused on giving me what for. Don't worry, though, I'll bring her around."

"How do you think you're going to do that? After the heated personal discussion, I mean?"

Gil grinned. "The *Gazette*'s running a profile on her and yours truly is doing the reporting."

"I thought you were an editor, these days."

"You know how it is at an operation like ours." Gil tucked his tongue into his cheek. "You pitch in where you need to."

"And you just happened to need to pitch in on a story about Jillian Logan."

"Coincidence is a wonderful thing," Gil said sunnily.

"I just bet. And did she fall for it?"

"Nope, she gave me the scratchy side of her mind."

"But?"

"I think she's getting a soft spot for me. She doesn't look at me, anymore, like she's hoping for my untimely demise."

"She's getting patient enough to wait for the timely version?" Alan asked.

"Something like that."

"I'd say you're in."

Gil gave a broad smile. "I will be."

"Where's your shadow?" Lois asked. Case files spread across the little table in her office as she and Jillian finished their regular Thursday afternoon status meeting.

"Gil's entertaining himself," Jillian said. "I told him we had work to do."

When Jillian and David had been newly adopted, Terrence and Leslie Logan had brought them to the Children's Connection for counseling. Still in her twenties, Lois had been the clinic's only social worker. She'd immersed herself in their case, spending hours working to help the two children get past the neglect and trauma they'd suffered. If Jillian had anything approaching a normal life, it was due as much to Lois as the Logans. It was because of Lois that Jillian had become a social worker, herself.

Over the years, Lois had morphed from counselor to mentor to colleague. And, throughout it all, friend. Next to David, Lois was most truly the one Jillian let into her life.

"So how are things going?"

"Well enough, I suppose." Jillian moved her shoulders. "It hasn't been as difficult as I expected."

"Interesting. I'd expect it would make you, of all people, uncomfortable to have someone around all the time."

"It has." Though not in the way she'd expected.

Lois gave her an assessing gaze. "Getting outside of your comfort zone isn't necessarily a bad thing. It's a good path to growth."

"Should I go sit on the couch?" Jillian asked in amusement.

"I'm not speaking as a therapist. I'm speaking as someone who cares about you. You cope better than anyone I know, Jillian. You've got a thriving career, a beautiful home. You're lovely, charming, socially adept. You had a traumatic early childhood but at a glance, you've transcended it." She paused.

"But?" Jillian prompted.

"But I wonder what happens when you shut the door behind you at night," she said softly.

Jillian glanced away. "I'm usually tired enough after work that all I want to do is relax."

"Life needs to be about more than work and re-covering from work. You're isolated, Jillian.

You've coped but you've never let yourself live your life. You're spectacularly good at letting people come close but no closer. So maybe the fact that this young man makes you uncomfortable is good. Because it's not just about work, is it?"

"I don't know what to do about him, Lois," Jillian blurted. "He scares me."

Lois merely waited, silent.

"It's too easy with him," Jillian continued in a low voice. "When I let it go, it moves too fast. It could turn into something if I let it."

"And then you'd be at risk."

Suddenly, the prospect seemed terrifying. She could hear her heartbeat thudding in her ears.

"You learned early not to trust," Lois said quietly. "That's a hard lesson to forget."

"I just don't want to be hurt," Jillian whispered.

"Don't you think it's as possible to hurt because you don't take risks? Take a chance, Jillian. You might just be surprised." Lois glanced at her watch. "Anyway, I think we're done here. Time to move on to the next thing, don't you think?"

When Jillian got back to her office, Gil was there, tapping away on his keyboard as usual. He blinked and shook his head as she walked up.

"You look like you're flagging a little," she said.

"If I don't pound a double espresso quick, I'm

going to go down for the count. I'm in serious need of caffeine. I saw a Stumptown down the street. I think I'm going to head over for a quick coffee run. Want anything? A skinny decaf latte with dry foam?"

Jillian considered. "How about a shot in the dark?"

"Coffee with a shot of espresso? I like a woman who's serious about her caffeine," he said, rising. "One shot in the dark, coming up."

"Thanks. I could use it."

"Maybe if you're really grateful you can finally give me that interview."

She remembered Lois. Maybe it was time. "Okay, let's do it."

"Seriously?"

"Bring me back the shot in the dark and we'll see."

She listened to him walk away and bent back to her work. Focus kept eluding her as the minutes went by. It wasn't lack of caffeine but excess nerves. Agreeing to an interview was one thing; the hard part was actually doing it.

"Open up," Lois had said, but she didn't understand how hard it was. She didn't know.

The phone burbled. Absently, eyes still on her report, Jillian reached for the receiver. "Hello?"

There was silence on the end of the line and she came to instant attention. "Hello?" she repeated.

"Robbie, is that you? Don't hang up," she said urgently. "Talk to me."

The seconds ticked by at the rate of her heartbeat. Her fingers tightened around the receiver. "Please? We're all so worried about you. We just want to know you're all right."

"I'm all right."

Jillian closed her eyes and let out a slow breath. "I'm glad you said something," she said. "Another minute and I was afraid I was going to find out I was having a conversation with an obscene phone caller."

His laughter sounded tense. "No, just Robbie the family screwup."

"You know that's not true."

"Yeah, well, it's not always easy to believe. How's Nancy?" he asked abruptly.

"She's holding on," Jillian said. "I won't lie to you—your leaving has been really hard on her. On all of us."

"Not much more than me staying around. I mean, come on, would you want to be married to a guy who showed up on the papers in the supermarket checkout counters?"

"Nancy knows that's not you and she knows those papers are wrong. We all do." And, oh, Robbie, she has something to tell you, something you have to know, Jillian thought with an ache in her throat. "Come back, Robbie. Before your probation officer finds out you're gone. The *Gazette* isn't running stories anymore. Things have cooled off."

"That's funny, I'm standing by a Kwik Stop mart and the *Messenger* has the usual article on me."

"You can't let the lies get to you."

"It's easier to say when you're not the person being lied about. Besides, they're not lies."

"They're not the truth, either. Come home," she pleaded. "If they find out you're gone—"

"I check in by phone. As far as Dawn's concerned, I'm present and accounted for."

"And if she finds out you're gone, you could go to jail," Jillian said. Part of her was truly angry with him for taking such an unnecessary chance. "Come back, Robbie. You can get through this with us."

"I'm never going to get away from this, not in Portland, not anywhere." His voice vibrated with frustration and something more. Hopelessness. "Face it, I'm always going to be the screwed-up babynapper."

"But Nancy—"

"Nancy's better off without me," he said bleakly. "Maybe everyone would be."

And then there was only the buzzing of the dial tone in her ear.

Gil walked into Jillian's office, carrying tray in hand. "One shot in the dark, coming up," he announced. "You didn't say anything about cream but I brought sugar and—"

Jillian wasn't listening. She wasn't even reacting. She was just staring at the wall, frozen, clutching the telephone receiver. Finally, like an automaton, she hung up.

Gil set the carrier on the edge of her desk. "Coffee?" he said, watching her closely.

Something had happened. She was rattled. He never thought he'd see it, but the calm, organized, unflappable Jillian was rattled and, unless he was very much mistaken, about ready to go to pieces.

"Everything okay?" he asked.

It was as though she'd been touched with an electrical shock. "Sure. Yeah. Fine," she said brightly, reaching for the cup. She started to take a drink and frowned, wiping off her hand.

He watched her carefully as he settled into the chair. "So is it still a good time to do the interview?"

She started to take another sip of her coffee and made a noise of frustration.

"What's wrong?" he asked gently.

"Nothing. The stupid lid's dripping." But her hand shook as she tried to get the plastic lid off and a startling splash of brown appeared on her cream silk blouse. "Dammit," she snapped.

He saw it as it was happening, too quick for him to warn her. One minute, she was hurrying to set the cup on her desk so she could wipe her blouse, the next, she'd knocked the bottom of the cardboard into the edge of the wood so that the cup tipped, sending a tide of steaming hot coffee across her desk.

"Oh, *no.*" Frantically, she stood bolt upright, snatching up files to rescue most of them from the spreading lake of coffee, splashing more spots on her cream blouse and trousers. For an instant, she stood indecisively as coffee streamed onto the carpet, scanning the room for a safe place to put the folders. Finally, she just grabbed at her trash can with her free hand, putting it under the edge of the desk to capture the waterfall of coffee, then falling to her knees with the tissue to mop up the spots, still holding the damp files.

"Forget about the carpet, what about your hand? Did you burn yourself?"

She shook her head and kept dabbing, then rose to start on the desk. "It doesn't matter," she said.

"Yes it does." He reached out to inspect the red spots on the back of her hand where the coffee had scalded her. "The furniture can wait."

"You don't understand." Her voice was tight with anxiety. "I've got to do something."

"Later."

"*Now.*" And before his astounded eyes, she dropped the files and burst into tears.

"Hey." He pulled her to him, wrapping his arms around her. He could feel her shaking, hear the hitch of her breath. "It's okay," he murmured, lips against her hair.

"No. It's not," she said, and the little broken note in her voice squeezed his heart.

"Shh." He smoothed a hand down her back. "Talk to me. Tell me what's wrong."

She moved her head. "I can't."

So for long moments he just stood, rocking her gently as she gradually calmed. "If you can't talk to me, is there someone else? Someone you can call?"

She tried to move away. "I'll be all right."

"Right now, you seem pretty damned far from all right. Just sit and let me take care of it. I'm going to get some paper towels and get up the rest of this coffee and then we're going to take you home."

Surprisingly, she didn't make a murmur of protest. She was silent on the drive to her house, speaking only to give him directions. Finally, he was parking at her curb. When he guided her up the steps by resting his hand lightly on her back, she didn't protest. And she didn't protest when he stood before her, his hands resting on her hips.

He nodded at her clothes. "Can you get those cleaned?"

She shrugged. "Probably not. It doesn't matter." The weeping was done. Now she just appeared pale and fatigued and drawn. She looked up at him. "You've been really nice tonight."

"I'm a nice guy."

A ghost of a smile drifted over her face. "I appreciate it."

"Then make it up to me."

"How?"

"Spend Sunday with me. Just you and me. No work, no baggage. Just a good time. What do you say?"

"A good time?"

"You know how, right?"

This time the smile was stronger. "All right."

"Good. I'll pick you up at ten. Wear shorts and tennis shoes."

"Shorts and tennis shoes? What are we going to do?"

He kissed the tip of her nose. "Have fun."

Chapter Ten

"How are you?" Jillian asked Alison gently. It was Friday evening. Three days earlier, the girl had been weeping in Jillian's office. Now, the anxiety still showed but her eyes remained dry.

"How am I? Terrified, actually. Crazy, panicked, trapped. Excited. Furious at myself. Something different every minute." She tried for a smile. "The variety pack."

"I know that feeling," Lisa Barrett said from the couch where she sat. "I was there. It's all normal."

Alison took in the neat pale-rose suit, the brisk, efficient air. "What do you do?"

"Property development," Lisa said. "I have a

business degree and I'm currently taking classes toward my MBA. How about you?"

Alison hesitated.

"Anything you say here is confidential, Alison," Jillian reminded her. "You can say as much or as little as you like, whatever makes you comfortable."

"I'm going to school for history. I wanted to teach but now I'm so afraid I've wrecked it all. I can't believe I've worked so hard all these years and then one night of being stupid, one night of not paying attention…"

"Nothing's wrecked." Lisa's voice was gentle. "You've got all kinds of choices. That was the main thing I learned when I came to the Children's Connection. I had choices and they'd help me no matter what."

"What would you do if you were me?" Alison asked.

"I can't say that because I'm not you. I made what I thought was the right decision for me at the time. Have I had regrets? Yes, some, but I'm still a part of Timothy's life. That's the important part."

Alison's fingers dug into the upholstery. "How did you know you were making the right decision?"

Lisa gave a sympathetic smile. "I didn't. All I could do, really, was hope."

"I'm so afraid I'm going to do something I'll be sorry for, no matter what I decide."

"Make a list of the pros and cons, think about it all. And then go with your gut. Just know that whatever you decide, Jillian and the Children's Connection will be there to help you." Lisa reached out to squeeze Alison's hand. "And call me anytime you need to talk."

Alison blinked back the shimmer of tears. "That's what Jillian said."

"It'll be okay, Alison," Lisa said softly. "You'll work out the right thing."

After, Lisa and Jillian sat in a Greek restaurant on the edge of Old Town. Bouzouki music played. The walls bore murals of olive groves and brilliant blue seas and dancers dressed in black and white and scarlet.

Lisa twirled her wineglass.

"How was your honeymoon?" Jillian asked.

"Wonderful," Lisa said. "Not long enough but we had a project we didn't want to leave hanging. We'll take a couple of weeks off at Christmas."

We. The two of them were already a unit, Jillian realized, cemented in some indefinable way that hadn't been possible two weeks before. Before the wedding.

Had it really been only two weeks? she wondered. So much had happened, so many subtle changes in her life.

"Why didn't you tell me about Gil?" she asked quietly.

Lisa suddenly became very busy with her napkin, folding and arranging it in her lap. "I didn't know what to do," she said finally. "I was afraid that it would ruin the whole weekend. Or that you'd refuse to be in the wedding and I really wanted you there." She met Jillian's gaze directly. "And Alan wanted Gil to be in it just as much. They've been friends since college."

"You didn't think I'd be able to understand that and go through the wedding, anyway? Give me some credit, Lisa. I'm a social worker. Dealing with emotions is what I do."

"This wasn't just dealing with emotions. The *Gazette* came after your family. You were furious about it."

"I'm still furious about it. That doesn't mean I can't separate the two."

"I just didn't know how to tell you."

Uncharacteristic anger flared. "You didn't think I deserved to be told so that I knew who I was dealing with?" So that she didn't wind up kissing him? So that she didn't wind up falling for him?

"I thought it would be all right," Lisa said miserably. "It was only the rehearsal and the wedding and it would be over. Alan made Gil promise he wouldn't say anything about the paper."

Jillian stared. "Alan made Gil…" she repeated.

"We just thought it was the best way to handle it," Lisa went on, not noticing. "We were wrong, Jillian. It seems really obvious now, but at the time I just couldn't see how it could ever work. It was just overwhelming. I was all in knots over the wedding and you were so angry and upset over Robbie."

And Jillian was still angry over Robbie, but things suddenly weren't so clear, somehow.

"We screwed up. I can't tell you how sorry I am that you found out the way you did."

Jillian shook her head, trying to take it all in. "So it wasn't Gil's idea to lie?"

Lisa winced at the words. "Alan asked him to say Blazon Media instead of the *Gazette*. It was the truth, just not all of it." She made a face. "And that sounds weak and lame, doesn't it? We were wrong. I was wrong. I should have been a better friend than that."

Something pretty much everyone alive could say, Jillian thought, especially at twenty-one. "It's okay, Lisa. Be straight with me next time but I get why it happened."

"I just don't want you to blame Gil for it. It wasn't his fault. He's a good guy. He tries to do the right thing."

"He could do better."

Something every person alive could say. Including her.

"I understand why you're so upset about Robbie," Lisa said. "I hated the paper when that news story came out about Thad and me. Alan called Gil to give him what for but then it turned out that Gil wasn't even here when it happened. He was on vacation. But he made it right when he got home, on his own. Before Alan ever talked to him."

The waiter brought their appetizers. Lisa waited until he'd set down tzatsiki and bread and left before speaking again. "Alan says he's interested in you."

Jillian rolled her eyes. "Are we in junior high now?"

Lisa ignored her comment. "You were as thick as thieves at the wedding. And with this shadowing thing you've been together nearly a week. What do you think of him?"

Too much, was what she thought of him. She thought of him too much. "Lisa, he was part of what chased Robbie away. How can I take anything seriously with him?"

"Take anything seriously with him or with anyone?"

"What's that supposed to mean?"

"You know, I always feel good when I talk with you." Lisa set her wine aside. "I always feel like we're close. And then I get home and realize that we spent most of the time talking about the clinic or your family or me. You never talk about you."

"I talk about myself," Jillian said uncomfortably.

"No, you don't. You're very good at it."

"Look, I don't know how we got from Gil to this. I've known him for all of two weeks."

"It took less than that for me to fall in love with Alan."

"First of all, there is no way I'm even close to being in love with Gil Reynolds," Jillian burst out. "I'm not even sure I like him." Oh, yes, you do, said a mocking voice in her head. "Look—" she softened her words with effort "—I'm really happy for you that you're so happy. And I'm flattered that you care about me. But you're looking for way more with Gil than is there. What happened with you and Alan was a one-in-a-million thing. Lightning doesn't strike twice."

"Looks to me like lightning's never struck you." Lisa scooped up some tzatsiki with her bread. "I'd say you're due."

The morning was clear and breezy, the air warm as Gil bounded up the steps to Jillian's porch. He rang the bell and waited, turning to see the details he hadn't noticed two days before.

The house was lovingly attended to, it was clear. White wicker porch furniture with fat, colorful cushions provided the perfect place to spend a lazy summer afternoon with a book. The flowers grew vibrant and healthy and tidy, without a leaf out of place. The switch plate around the doorbell was beaten copper. On the sidewalk across the street, a man and woman walked a corgi and what might charitably have been called a shepherd-terrier mix.

At a sound behind him, he turned to see Jillian on the other side of the screen.

"Morning," he said.

"Good morning."

She wore shorts and a top the color of raspberries. She'd pulled her hair back in a ponytail. She held a bright green watering can and watched him with a somewhat skeptical gaze.

"Ready to go?" he asked.

"Sure. I just have to get a few things." She hesitated and pushed at the screen latch. "Would you like to come in?"

It was curiosity that had him stepping inside. Big rooms, high ceilings, darker than most houses because of the spreading eaves. Fat sofas, warm wood that gleamed with polish. Lovingly cared for, he thought again, and scrupulously tidy, like her office. There was a sense of comfort, a warmth that had to do with more than just the temperature.

And whimsy. From the bottom of a light fixture

dangled a carved wooden hummingbird. A glass butterfly balanced on the top of the half-high wall that separated the living room from the hall. A small clutch of books was held in place by a pair of carved wooden beavers.

He followed her into the kitchen and she jumped when she turned to find him behind her. "Oh. I didn't realize…"

He caught her shoulders to steady her. Her lips were parted. Without her usual heels, she seemed smaller than he expected.

It took work to make himself release her.

The spotless kitchen was like something out of the Fifties, with butter-colored walls and gleaming white cabinets. A painted metal bread box dotted in red and blue and yellow sat on the counter, against the yellow-and-white tiled backsplash. The Formica and metal table in the breakfast nook held ceramic salt-and-pepper shakers shaped like grinning cows wearing hula skirts. At the window hung curtains patterned with dancing loaves of bread; violets sat on the sill, a green frog hanging on the edge of one.

"Just let me do this and we can go," Jillian said, emptying out the watering pot and upturning it on a tray. In her short-sleeved shirt, with her hair up, she looked girlish and young. The smooth professional shell was gone.

"All set," she said, taking up her keys from a hook in the hallway and reaching for her purse. "So where are we going?"

"Wait and see," Gil replied.

The morning was bright and clear, the streets still quiet. He headed toward the river.

She'd come because she'd made a promise to him. The memory of losing control the night of Robbie's phone call still mortified her. Somehow, though, Gil had made it all right. He'd been there for her. She hadn't felt weak and conspicuous, she'd felt…safe. She'd felt connected. And even though she knew it wasn't smart, she wanted more.

Besides, she owed him an apology.

It wasn't until they'd crossed the river and gone up an access road that Jillian had begun to get an idea of their destination. When she saw the forest of white masts, she was sure of it.

"Sailing?"

"Yeah." He glanced at her as he turned off his truck. "That all right?"

"As long as you don't expect me to know what I'm doing."

"Your job is to relax and enjoy yourself."

"That," she told him, "I can do."

"Good." He grinned, his teeth very white against his skin. He wore shorts and Top-Sider shoes, sunglasses and a short-sleeved shirt in a blue-green batik pattern. There was a buoyant energy to him that she'd never quite seen before. He was in his element, she realized.

The sleek white sloop bobbed at the dock, maybe fifteen feet long with gleaming brightwork and a glowing mahogany panel around the hatch to the belowdecks.

"The *Blueline?*" she said, reading the name.

He grinned. "She corrects what's wrong with me." Hopping down into the cockpit, he turned to offer her a hand. His palm was warm and sure against hers as she stepped down into the boat. He didn't release her at once. Instead, he stood, his hands now on her hips.

Jillian moistened her lips. "Shouldn't we get started?"

He raised a brow. "Sure. Just what do you want to start?"

She flushed. "I was talking about sailing."

"I wasn't." He flashed a smiled and released her. "But if you insist, I guess we need sails."

He opened up the hatch and ducked in to pull out bright blue cushions for the seats that ran along the sides of the cockpit, then a big grayish white canvas bag that presumably held the sails.

"Do you have bunks under there?" she asked.

"She can sleep two. If you don't mind being cozy," he added as he stepped up on the upper deck.

"She's a seventeen footer, though, really more for day trips. I just take her along the river, mostly."

"Can I help?" Jillian asked as he began putting up the sail.

"If you want to."

"Show me what to do."

So he showed her how to fix the sail on the boom and use the halyard to raise it up the mast. Once they'd gotten the jib up and Gil had given a push off the dock, the breeze was enough to move them.

"Why don't you use the motor to get out of the marina?" Jillian asked over her shoulder as she moved the sails under his direction so they could tack through the turns.

"Motors are for wimps," Gil said from where he sat back by the tiller. "It's called a sailboat for a reason."

"You're one of those guys who likes a challenge, aren't you?"

His glance was very direct. "I don't mind putting in a little effort when it's for something I want."

The eye contact lasted a few beats longer than it should have, a few beats during which she was very conscious of the fact that the cockpit was only three or four feet long and that his thigh was mere inches from where her hand rested on the cushion.

And then they were out of the marina and into open water, the breeze fresh in her face.

"We'll go upriver to Ross Island and then cut back," he said. "Okay with you?"

"Aye, aye, Captain." She saluted him smartly.

The wind was strong enough to tease up small whitecaps, making the boat leap over the water. The speed was exhilarating. Along the east bank, she could see the esplanade. To the west, beyond the greensward of Tom McCall Park, rose the buildings of the downtown.

"It all looks so different from here," she said as they passed the pilings of the Marquam Bridge.

"Funny how things always look different depending on where you're sitting."

She slanted him a quick look. "Editorial comment?"

"Observation."

They worked their way up the river to the midstream teardrop of Ross Island. A great blue heron stalked along the shore of the island, the picture of affronted dignity. "They always make me think of those old pictures of businessmen and bankers in the nineteen hundreds," said Gil. "You know, the ones with the starched collars and monocles."

Jillian laughed. "They'd have to have very long trousers."

"I'll say."

They came about a bit above the island. As they

watched, first one, then another, then another of the herons launched itself into the air, like some kind of avian drill team, until they were soaring along the river with ponderous flaps of their wings.

"They're so beautiful when they're in the air," Jillian murmured. Impulsively, she reached over and squeezed Gil's hand where it rested on the royal-blue cushion beside her. "This is wonderful. Thank you so much for bringing me."

"I'm glad you like it." He moved his hand to clasp hers. "I wanted you to see it."

Jillian watched the approaching arch of the Ross Island Bridge. "I talked to Lisa," she said, turning back to him. "She told me that the Blazon media thing wasn't you, that she and Alan asked you to say it."

"We're not talking about any of that today, remember?"

"I need to. Why didn't you tell me it wasn't you?" Why had he let her think he had chosen to lie?

He seemed embarrassed. "I agreed to do it. It was a stupid choice but the minute I made it, it was my responsibility."

"It wasn't your idea, though."

He adjusted the tiller. "I wasn't going to cry off because of that. I don't work that way."

He wouldn't, she realized. She might not always agree with his decisions, but she was beginning to realize that the decisions he made were honorable by the terms of his code.

She looked at the downtown in the distance. "You're right," she said. "Things do look different depending on where you're sitting. How far are we going?"

His gaze on hers was steady. "As far as we can," he said.

The sun was setting as they walked down Glison Street in the Pearl. The long, lazy sail had given way to a lunch so late it was practically an early dinner. Now, they wandered from gallery to gallery, mostly as an excuse to keep talking. Neither was ready for the day to end.

"Do you think the heat got too high and they melted?" Jillian studied the cluster of sculptures before her. They'd started out as narrow green pyramids about the height of a bowling pin but instead of tapering to sharp points, the tips bent in free-form curves like spires of melting wax.

"I don't know," Gil said, pacing around them. "I like them, though. They'd go really well in my condo."

"What's your condo like?" Jillian asked. "Industrial, I'm guessing, or maybe Italian."

"You could see for yourself if you want. We're only about two blocks away."

"Really?"

"Sure. Come in for a drink and a tour. I'll drive you home after." When she hesitated, he smiled. "No strings," he promised. "You'll be perfectly safe. Give me a minute, though. I want to buy these guys."

She wandered around the rest of the gallery while he completed the purchase, admiring a flame-colored glass vase and staring with wrinkled brow at what might have been a funerary mask for a wild boar, tusks and all.

Half an hour later, they were back on the street, headed to his condo.

It made her nervous to be heading to his space. Silly, she chided herself as they rode the elevator up. It wasn't as if she was going to stay long, just go in for a quick drink. They'd spent the day together—shoot, they'd spent the week—and one thing she knew by now was that they weren't likely to run out of things to say.

The condo wasn't decorated in industrial or Italian. It was a quietly modern loft with sleek, clean-lined furniture in blond wood and brushed aluminum. The walls were exposed brick, the floors polished maple, the ceilings high. Kitchen and living room occupied the ground floor; a curving staircase led up to what she presumed was his bedroom.

"How long have you lived here?" Jillian asked, drifting over to the sliding-glass door that let out onto his balcony.

"Four years," he answered from behind the counter that separated out the space that was his kitchen. "I got in just about the time the neighborhood was starting to go upscale."

"Can you see the river from here?"

"A slice. Along with the container-loading equipment at the port." He paused. "Maybe I should have gone for industrial. Anyway, what can I get you to drink? I've got wine, beer, vodka. Even a bottle of brandy, I think."

"Red wine would work."

He picked up a bottle and glanced at it. "Red zin okay?"

She nodded. "So where are you going to put the sculpture?" she asked, taking the glass he handed to her.

"On the coffee table," he answered, moving aside the wide glass bowl that currently sat there. "Let's get them out and see how they look."

He brought over the bag from the gallery and began pulling out the cardboard-and-tissue-wrapped pyramids and laying them side by side.

Jillian walked over to help, first standing, then perching beside him.

"No wonder it took forever for you to buy

these," she muttered, fighting to break off ring after ring of tape.

Tissue paper rustled as he stripped it off and set a pyramid on the table. "It wasn't the buying, darlin', it was the wrapping."

"I see that. It's beginning to look like Christmas in here," she observed, looking at the growing pile of paper next to the table.

"Oh, speaking of which—" he dug in the bag and pulled out a small box "—here."

Jillian blinked. "For me? Why?"

He considered. "Because it's a Sunday? Open it." He went back to unwrapping the last pyramid.

It was a small recycled paper box with a band about it. When she opened the lid, she pulled out a small bundle. She unwrapped the tissue paper inside to reveal a delicate glass dragonfly hanging from a golden cord.

"Oh, Gil." She breathed.

"You like it?"

"Of course I like it. It's beautiful." She held it up so that it turned and caught the light.

"I thought it would go with your humming-birds and things."

He'd noticed, she thought, shaken. He'd been in her house perhaps ten minutes and he'd seen. She set the dragonfly down. "That was really sweet of you."

He caught her hand and brought it to his lips. "I have my moments," he said, lingering over her knuckles, her fingertips, eyes watching her.

And the breath backed up in her lungs. His eyes were intent on hers. She stared into them and suddenly she was falling into that hot, dark gaze, falling into the heat, falling into him until her world reduced to those dark pools and the warmth of his lips on her hand. Her world reduced to him. And somewhere deep inside her, a slow beat of desire began to pulse.

He turned up her hand to kiss her palm. She made a soft, helpless sound. Her fingers curved around his cheek, the slight roughness of his beard counterpointing the softness of his mouth. Then he turned her wrist to press his lips against the tender skin on the inside where her pulse beat, making her shiver a little.

And he leaned in to take her mouth with his.

It wasn't the tentative exploration of their first kiss, nor the urgent, reckless demand of the second. Instead, it was confident possession, patient with the knowledge that, this time around, there was time enough. Their other kisses had been snatched in the open, standing, grasping, waiting for interruption. Here, now, there was to be no disturbance. Here, it was just the two of them with all the time in the world to concentrate, to savor, to find all that a kiss could give.

He kissed her as though he'd be content to just browse on her mouth endlessly, now nipping, now dipping deep. He was touch, taste. Seduction. And, oh, it was extravagant, glorious to lean back against the soft cushions of the couch and immerse herself in him.

His flavor seeped into her, the tartness from the wine overlaying a more complex flavor that was purely male. And Jillian took what she'd learned from him, changing the angle of the kiss, rubbing her lips against his until he was the one who made an impatient noise and pressed harder against her.

Time became immaterial. Long minutes slid by with the sound of breath, the feel of mouth on mouth, the smoothing of hand over skin. Pleasure rippled through her.

When his hand ran up her bare thigh, she felt the trail of desire. It had been so long since she'd felt the touch of another. In delight, she felt him break the kiss and begin to explore her face, nibbling his way up her cheek to drop kisses on her eyelids, cruising down along her jaw. And then he dipped lower, pressing his lips to the long line of her throat.

She'd never known her skin could be so sensitive. The kiss had generated pleasure but this was something different. This evoked a dark heat somewhere deep inside her. Instinctively, she let her head fall back while he feasted on her, pressing his lips to the hollow at the base of her neck. And dropping lower.

A slow tension began to build in her and she twisted against him. The heat of his mouth moving down her chest into the vee of her open collar brought her closer to the peak of desire. His hand moved up over her hip, then along her side and up to cover her breast.

This was it, Jillian thought to herself. This was the time. She'd waited too long, she'd lived on the outside. This was her chance to join the rest of the human race.

And she slid her arms around him.

He tugged at her shirt, slipping it out from her shorts so that he could move his hand beneath it to slide possessively up over her breast. She could feel the heat of his hand through the cloth of her bra. Then his mouth went lower, pushing her shirt aside, licking the fragile skin on top of her breast. And arousal dragged her down into hot wanting until her hips were moving without volition, until she was gasping and straining against him, until she was desperate with the desire for more. Until she was—

Out of control.

And suddenly the good tension shifted somehow, pleasure lost, morphing into agitation, anxiety. Suddenly, her chest felt tight with panic and she broke the kiss, pushing away.

"What's wrong?" Gil asked, trying to just hold her but every nerve in her body was now screaming to get loose.

"Let me up. Let me up," she said breathlessly. "I need *up*."

She stood and walked across the room, panting as though she'd just run a mile. Blindly, she stared out the window to the lights across the river. Where home was. Behind her, she heard only silence, then the sound of Gil standing and walking across to her.

"What's going on?" he asked quietly.

"I just—" How could she tell him nothing? Or nothing that she knew of. She knew he expected a story, some grand trauma like they showed in the movies. How could she tell him that there was nothing she remembered, only the panic that hung in the wings. She moved her shoulders. "I'm sorry."

He came up behind her, put his hands on her shoulders. And she flinched before she could stop herself. "Okay," he said stepping back.

"I'm sorry," she said again, her voice shaking. "I should go."

"Just let me say one thing, okay? You're special, Jillian. I mean that. What we're doing here—" He was silent for a long time. "This matters to me," he said finally. "Tell me what's going on."

"I don't *know* what's going on," she said, a thread of desperation in her voice.

"Did someone hurt you?"

She whirled and stalked back to the couch. "I told you I don't—"

Any words she might have said were cut off by an electronic bleat that she recognized as her cell phone. She crossed to the kitchen breakfront and her purse, relieved at the interruption. With shaking hands, she pulled out the phone and flipped it open. "Hello?"

"Jillian?"

"Eric?" He sounded odd, she thought, his voice tense and higher than usual. "Is everything okay?"

"I think so. I hope so."

"What do you mean you hope so?"

"Get yourself down to Portland General. Jenny's having her baby."

Chapter Eleven

Gil pulled up to the front of the hospital emergency room area and stopped. Portland General was a matter of blocks away from his condo. Taking Jillian directly there instead of back to her house in Ladd's Addition had simply made sense.

Even though the last thing he wanted to do just then was let her go.

"Are you sure you're going to be okay?" he asked.

"Of course." Her response was too quick. She didn't look at him.

She wasn't okay. Nothing was okay. One minute, she'd been like a naked flame in his arms. The next, she'd shut down and the air was thick with tension. Something was very wrong but he was damned if he knew what.

And he was damned if he knew how to get at it.

"I'd go in with you but I don't want to get lynched by a pack of Logans."

The smile came and went too quickly. "We're not that dangerous."

"Want to bet? Probably best if I leave you to it. Call me when you need a ride home, okay?"

"Thanks for the offer but it could take all night, you just never know. I have a lot of family here. I'm sure someone can give me a lift." She hesitated. "Thank you for today. The dragonfly is lovely."

"No problem." He watched her as she opened the door. "I had a good time."

"Me, too." She did look at him then, her eyes dark and enormous.

Even as he lectured himself to give her space, he reached out and brushed her hair back from her face. "Take care. Give my best to your sister-in-law."

And he watched her walk away.

As the lights of the hospital faded behind him, Gil shook his head. She'd made it clear that she wanted to be as far away from him as she could. She was going to be okay, he told himself, she was going to be with her family. But something in the set of her shoulders had looked fragile and vulnerable as she'd stepped through the sliding doors to the emergency room.

No matter how much everything in him rebelled at leaving her while things were still so up in the air, now wasn't the time. And a part of him, he didn't want to admit, felt relief at not having to face her family.

He'd always done his best to live an honest life. Not perfect, by any means. After all, there had been the incident of the plaster of paris and the history teacher's Thermos, but that had been in junior high. Overall, he'd always done his best to live a life that he didn't have to make excuses for.

And yet somehow, obscurely, he felt that he needed to now. Even though he stood by the *Gazette*'s coverage of Robbie Logan, it was a break not to have to walk into that hospital with Jillian and create a mess.

Because the reality was, it could be. Suddenly, he was putting a personal face to the news, always a dangerous thing for a newsman. Sure, there had been one with Lisa's story, but the damage done hadn't been by his hand; he'd been able to correct things.

In the case of Robbie Logan, the situation was far more ambiguous. Now, Gil had begun to see the damage his coverage could do to people's lives. To Jillian's life. Now, the journalistic remove he'd always prized had begun to evaporate. Sure things were quiet right now but there would be more stories, and not just Jillian's profile. How would he do his job at the paper? How would he make the decision on whether to run a Robbie Logan story or not, knowing that it could disturb the fragile connection forming between him and Jillian?

What was between them wasn't done, not by half. She wasn't just another woman; what he felt for her was strong and real. He'd already known there were secrets. He'd sensed them even before the incident in his condo. She'd been hurt, some way, somehow. One moment, she'd been heat and excitement, her mouth avid against his. The next, she'd been tense and withdrawn. Something was going on, something they needed to talk about, but the barriers she'd put up were thick and high.

And he had to find the patience to get around them.

Time, he told himself. Time, pure and simple.

The birthing room looked more like a bedroom suite in a nice hotel. Correction, Jillian thought as she walked in, it looked more like a nice hotel suite where a reception was being held. She'd always known she was part of a large family, but there were easily over a dozen people milling around the room, flopped on the sofas and chairs, standing by the window and using their cell phones.

Eric sat by the bed holding Jenny's hand while Eden stood on the other side, dabbing perspiration off Jenny's forehead. Jenny's brother, Jordan, sprawled in a chair near the foot of the bed, a magazine open on his knees, Sarajane standing behind him.

Jillian made her way over to Jenny. "Hi, hon. So what's going on?"

Jenny's eyes were bright with excitement. "I'm having a baby, haven't you heard?"

"I see that," Jillian said. "Everything okay, mother-to-be? Anything you need?"

"Are you kidding? I've got half the staff of the Children's Connection here helping out."

"Is the offer good for the father-to-be?" Eric asked hopefully. "I could use a shot in the dark."

"Your whole life is a shot in the dark," Jordan cracked. "If you decide to have mercy on him and make a coffee run, though," he said to Jillian, "I'll take a latte."

"There's coffee in the break-room vending machine," Jillian pointed out.

Jordan winced. "I don't think you can call what's available around here coffee. Creosote, maybe."

"So I suppose you're expecting me to go on a mission of mercy," Jillian said.

"Well, expecting's probably overstating the case," Eric said. "Wishing, maybe. Hoping."

"We're just saying if you're feeling like doing something for the greater good, that would be it," Jordan clarified.

"If you want to take a run, I'll go with you," David said from beside her.

Jillian jumped. "When did you get here?"

"About two seconds ago. And I could seriously use some caffeine. Besides, I'm no good at just sitting around."

"Hello?" Jenny complained. "Remember who's been stuck in a bed for three months? I'm the one who's going nuts. You have no idea how ready I am to get up out of this bed."

"It'll be over soon," Eden soothed.

"I know. And first thing tomorrow I start training for the Portland marathon."

"You might want to give it a week or two," Jordan advised.

Jillian checked her watch. "You might also want to get the whole labor and birth thing out of the way. Considering tomorrow is only three hours away," she added.

Jenny waved a hand. "I'm not worried about this pesky labor stuff. I'm tougher than—" The words turned into a surprised little bleat as her face tensed and reddened. Sudden beads of sweat sprang out on her brow.

"Come on, honey, breathe," Eric said anxiously, looking a bit tense and red-faced himself.

Jenny gave a little moan. Each second seemed to take an eternity. Finally, the contraction ended and Jenny melted back into the mattress, gasping.

Eric opened and closed his hand a few times experimentally. "You've got quite a grip there."

"Just wait," Eden advised. "Trust me, she's just getting started."

"I think I'm going to miss our racquetball game next week, Jordan," Eric said. "Unless you give me a handicap."

"You're a walking handicap," Jordan tossed back. "Why else do you think you've managed to win any of our games?"

Jillian watched as Eden dabbed Jenny's brow. "So what was that you were saying about pesky labor?"

"I want drugs," Jenny said positively. "Really good drugs."

"Remember your Lamaze training," Eden advised, dabbing a sweetly scented oil on Jenny's temples. "The aromatherapy will help."

"A saddle block will help more," Jenny shot back. There was a musical laugh behind them and lovely, dark-eyed Alicia Juarez, Scott's fiancée, walked up wearing a smock decorated with cats and dogs holding umbrellas. "The doctor will be in to take care of it in just a couple of minutes."

"Bless you," Jenny said.

"If I were you, though, I'd still pay attention to Eden. Her techniques work. It's just if they don't, all the way, you'll have a backup."

"Backups are good," Eric said, flexing his hand again.

Alicia pulled the drape around the bed. "Okay, shoo, all of you except Eden. I need to check progress."

Obediently, Jillian and the rest stepped away and let Alicia get to work.

"Have we got everyone on the list?" Jillian asked David, who'd been taking coffee orders.

"I think so. Ready to go?"

He reached out for the door just as it opened to reveal Lawrence and Abby Logan.

For a moment, everyone froze, including Terrence in the corner, including Jillian. Her father and her uncle had reconciled, but a few conversations couldn't possibly repair the damage of years. Would her father consider Lawrence's appearance a positive gesture or would he consider it intrusive and condescending?

Terrence looked over, surprise writ large on his

face. There was a moment of hesitation and then he walked over, his hand extended. "Larry. Good to see you."

"Terrence. I heard that Jenny was going into labor. We just wanted to stop by and see if we could help. You know, best wishes, moral support, all that. I guess you have plenty of that, though."

Jillian held her breath.

"We can always use more," Terrence said. "Our family makes time for one another."

Lawrence studied him. "You're right, we Logans do."

"Stay." It was Jenny's voice, from the bed. "Nathan should be born with his family around. All his family."

"Jenny's right," Terrence said. "Stay."

And around the room, everyone subtly relaxed. Except one.

"Nathan?" Eric repeated plaintively. "I thought we'd decided on Joe."

"Would you ever in a million years have thought it?" David and Jillian headed back from Stumptown balancing carriers of coffee.

"You mean Dad and Uncle Lawrence? I'd hoped," Jillian answered. "I never really knew whether it would happen or not. Maybe it really will stick."

"Maybe. If it does, you deserve a lot of the credit."

"It wasn't just me. It was Jake and LJ. It was Mom. It was you. A lot of us made it happen." The hospital's automatic glass doors swished open and they stepped inside.

"Well, cheers to all of us. What matters is that it worked out. So what's going on with you?" David asked. "You look like you got some sun today."

Jillian could feel her cheeks heating. She could see it in the big round convex mirror up by the corridor ceiling that orderlies used to check for traffic before they took gurneys around corners.

"I was out sailing today."

"Oh, yeah?" He cocked a brow. "Anyone I know? Like the guy who was dropping you off when I drove up?"

Jillian slanted a look at him. "Aren't I a little old for you to be playing protective brother?"

"I don't know, do you need protecting?"

Just then, she felt as though she needed to be protected against herself, but she wasn't about to say that to David. "I think I can take care of myself."

"It's him, isn't it?" he said. "The guy from the paper?"

Slowly, she nodded.

"Is that why he didn't come in?"

"It was our first…" Was date even the right

word? "It was the first time we'd done anything together outside of work. He didn't need to come in and face the family."

"Especially given what he does for a living."

"Especially that. He doesn't need a black eye from Dad."

David grinned. "Dad would be more likely to sabotage his credit score than pop him one."

"Even so."

"So how'd it go? Good time?"

She could feel the box with the dragonfly in her pocket as she walked along. "Wonderful. At least, mostly."

"Mostly," he repeated. "You're covering well but you're looking a little rough around the edges. What happened?"

What had happened was that she'd failed once more. What had happened was that she'd been reminded, yet again, how screwed up she truly was. "Nothing I'm ready to talk about," she said. "I need to try to understand it myself."

"I thought you liked this guy. Did he turn into a jerk?"

"No. It wasn't him."

"Did you turn into a jerk?"

She snapped her head around to stare at him as they stepped into the elevator. "Whose side are you on, anyway?"

"Yours. Always yours. But you're not the easiest of people, Jilly."

Her brows lowered. "It was just life kind of stuff. I'll survive."

"Are you going to see him again?"

"I don't know." She moved her shoulders. "I don't know if he'll want to."

"He'd be an idiot if he didn't."

Jillian gave him a grateful smile. "Thanks."

"Like I said, I'm always on your side."

They stepped out on the obstetrics floor and headed down to Jenny's birthing suite. Alicia came bustling past them.

"How is she?" Jillian asked.

"She's five centimeters dilated. I think we're going to have a baby on our hands pretty soon." There was a cry from another room and she gave an apologetic smile. "I have to go check that."

When Jillian and David walked into the birthing room, it seemed to her that the crowd was even bigger than ever. And then she saw Nancy there and realized why. Jillian wondered if only she could see the lines of strain in Nancy's face. She still hadn't told the family about the baby. Being here, seeing Jenny, missing Robbie had to be killing her.

Unobtrusively, Jillian wandered casually over to where she stood by the windows, staring out into the darkness.

"You don't have to be here," Jillian said softly.

"I want to be." Nancy took a breath. "I need to be. I need to remind myself that there's family here, that Robbie's going to come home. It's going to be all right, isn't it? Tell me it's going to be all right."

"It *is* going to be all right. You'll see."

"I'm almost three months along and he still doesn't know. If he knew he'd come home. But…"

"He needs to come home on his own," Jillian finished for her.

"Not for obligation," Nancy said. "I want to tell him and it's selfish because I know it would bring him home. But it wouldn't be for the right reason. And maybe he'd stay for a while." She blinked, her voice wavering. "And maybe he would go again. Maybe not until his probation ends, but he'd go. I don't think I could bear it."

"He loves you, Nancy," Jillian said gently. "He's just got some things that he's got to work out. We can help but we can't do it for him."

"But when Scott finds him…"

"When Scott finds him, then we'll decide what happens next. No matter what's going on, he's got to come home to deal with his legal obligations. And maybe while he does, we can help with those demons he's fighting. And maybe everyone here can help you."

Nancy turned to look at the roomful of chattering people that made up the extended family she'd married into. The family she hadn't ever quite been able to convince Robbie he deserved.

"Tell them, Nancy. Let them share."

"But it's Jenny's moment. I don't want to steal her thunder."

"Jenny's not like that. And trust me, in about half an hour, you wouldn't be able to steal her thunder with a winning lottery ticket. A new baby trumps pretty much everything." Jillian gave Nancy a soft glance. "And the next best thing is one on the way."

Nancy gave her a long look and then nodded and turned to the room.

"Everybody," she said, "there's something I want to share with you all."

Chapter Twelve

Jillian wasn't sure how it had come to be Thursday afternoon already. The week had seemed to pass in a blur and at the same time to crawl by. She found herself thinking of Gil constantly, yet the thought of contacting him paralyzed her.

And from his end, the phone had stayed resolutely silent. Could she really blame him? She'd freaked out, then she'd bolted. What was he supposed to do? What was he supposed to think? He was a successful, charming, talented, good-looking guy. Why should he be spending his time with a basket case?

She made an impatient noise and gathered up

her files. Dwelling on it wasn't going to do anything except make her crazy.

Instead, she plastered on a smile and walked into Lois's office for their weekly meeting. "Hi."

Lois took one look at her face and set her own case files aside. "I could make small talk but we've known each other too long for that. What's wrong? Anything you want to talk about?"

Jillian gave a brief smile. "I finished my therapy five years ago. It's not your job anymore."

"I'm not being your therapist. I'm being a friend. What's going on? Is it your young man?"

Jillian shuffled the files she held, reorganizing them. Finally, she looked up. "We went out last weekend. Sailing."

"How was it?"

"Great. It was really a wonderful day. He's… easy," she decided. "Being with him isn't work like it is with other people. I feel like I can talk to him and he understands. We connect."

"Ah. So what happened?"

Jillian sighed. "We started kissing. Things got kind of hot and heavy."

"How was it?"

"Pretty amazing, actually. It's never been quite like that before. I just wanted more. And I started thinking that maybe this was it, this was the time it would be right."

"And?"

"I froze up," she said miserably. "One minute, I was into it and the next I was panicking. I just had to get out." She let out a long breath and turned to the window. "Anyway, I'm sure he thinks I'm way too screwed up to deal with. Since Sunday I haven't heard a word from him."

"Did you talk with him about what happened?"

"I couldn't. I didn't know what to talk about. What am I supposed to say, I'm thirty-three years old and a virgin? It sounds like the setup for a bad joke."

"You need to tell him about it before things go any further," Lois said gently. "He deserves to know."

"Maybe things aren't going to go any further," Jillian said. "Maybe what I do is chalk it up to a good run and try to do better next time." She glanced at her watch. "Anyway, I thought we were supposed to be reviewing case files."

"We are. It's an old one. Yours." Lois leaned forward. "You need to tell him, Jillian. Don't just walk away from this. You need your life to be whole."

"Maybe I just don't like sex," she tossed out, an edge in her voice.

"And maybe you saw something when you were a child, still with your mother," Lois countered. "I'm not talking overt abuse, touching or anything. It could have been as simple as walking in on a porn movie or seeing a couple having sex in the street."

"Why don't I remember?"

"It was thirty years ago. When you first came to the Children's Connection, maybe I didn't ask the right questions. I was looking for overt abuse. This could be more subtle. You know how deep preverbal memories can be buried, especially if it's something that doesn't seem like a transgression. If no one touched you, you probably wouldn't register it as an invasion but the effect could be just as strong. Do you mind if I try something?"

"If you're talking about hypnosis," Jillian said, "it never worked for me."

"I wouldn't expect it to. You're far too self-contained to ever allow yourself to be hypnotized. That requires a level of trust that you learned young wasn't safe. No, this is a sensory thing." Lois turned back to her desk and dug in the drawer. "I've had this for ages but there never seemed like a good time to bring it out. I hope I didn't just toss it sometime. Aha!" She flourished something triumphantly.

Jillian frowned at the square in Lois's hand. It was one of those glossy little cardboard folders that held a small sample bottle of perfume.

"It's Opium," Lois said. "Very popular in the

seventies. I picked it up because of something you said once about your mother. Smell it."

Sudden nerves gripped her. She didn't want to do this, oh, she didn't want to. But she made herself go through with it, she made herself pull out the plastic stopper and sniff.

Sweet and heavy, almost musky. Familiar, in a way that touched a chord. And, for an instant, something flashed in her mind: a flickering television, drunken laughter and bodies moving around on the couch.

The little tube fell out of her fingers, releasing a bloom of scent into the room.

"What?" Lois was watching her alertly.

Jillian shook her head. "I don't know."

"What image popped up?"

"I don't know," Jillian responded sharply.

"But you remembered something."

"Did I? Or did I just respond to your suggestion?"

"What was it?" Lois asked softly.

"My mother, with a man. Both of them naked. They were having sex. Loud, rough sex."

"Was she in distress?"

She didn't want to think about it but she made herself, spurred on by the light scent in the room. "I don't think so. I don't know. He had her bent over the couch. She was crying out."

"Like she was being hurt. You fear losing

control, Jillian. You always have. And for as long as I've known you, you've been jumpy about people coming up on you from behind. It makes sense now, doesn't it?"

The imagery wouldn't leave her head. Or the horrible equation formed by the child's mind—if she dropped her guard, if she gave into arousal, she would be the naked woman being hurt.

"So how do I get past it?"

"Understanding is a part, but you know as well as I do that that only goes so far. Past a certain point, you just have to make yourself trust. You have to demonstrate to yourself that the possibility you fear isn't the reality. With the right man, you could."

"Gil?" she whispered.

Lois gave her a tender look. "Only you know the answer to that. Whoever it is, you're going to have to tell him. He'll need to know what he's up against."

"Tell him what, that I'm hopelessly screwed up?"

"You're not hopelessly screwed up and you know it. You cope better than any trauma survivor I've ever seen. But life's about more than coping, isn't it? More than doing well at work. Don't you deserve something more? And doesn't he? You've got Gil operating in the dark right now. He doesn't know why you're pulling back. You need to trust him enough to at least tell him that, Jillian."

"But what if I can't? What if he doesn't want

to listen, can't understand? What if he's already decided that he wants no part of me?"

"Do you believe that?"

"I don't know."

"And there's no way you will know until you try." Lois smoothed a hand down her cheek. "Talk to him, Jillian. You owe it to both of you."

Gil sat at work, ostensibly staring at his computer screen. In reality, he was staring into space. He'd been doing that a lot since the weekend.

He glanced at the phone again, fighting the temptation to pick it up and call Jillian. Every cell of his body protested at not doing it. He was a person of action, always more comfortable doing. For more than twenty years, the theme of his life had been when in doubt, pick up the phone and start making moves. Usually, that meant pursuing a source.

In this case, it meant calling Jillian.

He'd cheerfully have done it if he'd thought it would do any good but he wasn't sure it would. What was going on with her wasn't to do with him and she'd made it abundantly clear that she didn't want to share the issue. Which gave him a choice. He could ignore her obvious wishes and press her, anyway, or he could give her her space and let her decide when to get in touch with him.

He'd gone with leaving it up to her. It had been

his only choice, really, he'd reasoned, because if she didn't open up to him out of choice, they didn't really have much of a chance, anyway. Now, though, four days later, he was having second thoughts.

In a way, it was just another set of the boundaries she surrounded herself with. They'd talked, sure, but about politics, movies, music, things happening in Portland. Sometimes, she would relax and it was just fun, no picking his way, no mysteries, just feeling good, laughing together. Like the day they'd sailed on the Willamette. But whenever the talk turned to her, Jillian had always adroitly managed to shift it to another topic.

And he understood it but he'd grown continually more frustrated. He wanted to get past the shutters. There was so much strength and compassion to her but then there was the vulnerability that lay beneath, the suddenly frantic woman who'd struggled against him like a trapped bird. He needed to give her time, he knew it, and yet he wanted her so much it was like rocks in his gut.

They'd never gotten around to the promised interview. In some ways, he felt he knew her deeply by watching. In other ways, he wondered if he knew her at all.

And he wondered how you built a relationship with someone who kept you always on the outside.

At the tap on his door, he glanced up to see Mark Fetzer, one of his beat writers. "What's up?"

"Got a minute?" Fetzer asked. "I've got a late-breaking story."

"We just finished the afternoon news planning meeting."

"Well, you're going to want to make space, especially if you're carrying that Seattle baby-kidnapping story."

"Why?"

"Robbie Logan's disappeared."

Conflict hovered over Doug and Shelly Dolan as they faced Jillian for their weekly session. They sat now at different ends of the sofa, Shelly with her arms wrapped around herself. The tension between them was palpable. "I want to try another implant," she said. "I know it didn't work last time but I want to try it again. And Doug doesn't want to but he won't talk about why. He says money but that's not it. He won't tell me. He never tells me. He keeps it all bottled up inside. He won't talk to anyone."

"I talk," Doug said.

"No, you don't," she flared. "I never know what you're thinking. I feel like I'm the only one who's going through this. I feel every day like I'm being sliced open but I say something to you and you just grunt."

"I don't grunt."

"You do. It's like I'm making a big deal out of nothing and you just wish I'd shut up."

"You want to know what I think?" he burst out. "I want my wife back. I want my marriage back. I am so sick of everything being about making a baby. I want to be out somewhere with you and see a stroller or a pregnant woman and not start worrying about how to keep you from seeing it, or how you'll react if you do. I want to go through one month without being in a cold sweat when it's time for your period." The words tumbled out. "I want to make love to my wife with only the two of us there, not the calendar and the thermometers and the doctors and the invisible baby floating around over it all."

He slammed his hand down on the couch arm. "We've been trying to do this for so long that it's not about us, anymore. Isn't that the whole reason we wanted to have children in the first place, because we loved each other and wanted to give that kind of a home to a kid? What the hell kind of a home do we have now, huh? It's baby, baby, baby, all the time. Aren't we enough for each other?" he pleaded. "What, if you don't have a baby you don't want me anymore? Is that all I'm good for?"

He rose and stalked to the windows, hands on his hips, frustration vibrating through him. "It's supposed to be about us."

"It is about us," Shelly said, tears streaming down her cheeks. "We've got so much to give."

"Hell, we can't even give to each other right now. All we can do is obsess over the schedule. And every month I watch you and it just destroys me because there's nothing I can do to fix it, there's nothing I can do to protect you. I'm supposed to be a man and I can't do my part."

"It's not you, we know that. It's me."

Doug crossed to the couch and folded Shelly into his arms. "Honey, you're perfect. You always have been. But this baby stuff is tearing us apart and I can't do it anymore. And I can't stand by and watch you do it to yourself."

"We've got so much love to give," she whispered.

"Then let's give it. I don't give a damn if it's got my nose or your eyes. All I want is to be a dad, to watch a kid grow, to play catch, to do the fun stuff and the hard stuff and make a family."

"That's what I want, too."

"Then forget about the fertility treatments and the shots and the schedules. Let's adopt. Jillian will help us with that," he said, staring at her almost angrily. "Won't you?"

* * *

She stood by her window and watched them leave the clinic together, walking across the street, Doug with his hand on the small of Shelly's back. They would be okay, Jillian thought. They'd reached the moment of crisis and come together. There was more work to be done, but they'd get through it.

Because they were a unit.

At the far side of the street, the two of them stopped before their car. Doug opened the door for her. Shelly turned to touch his cheek and then suddenly they were pressed together, hugging one another and kissing as though they'd fly apart if they only let go.

And sudden longing knifed through Jillian. That was what made life worth having, that connection, that trust, that absolute intimacy. And abruptly she found herself yearning for Gil.

Tell him, Lois had said.

Three weeks before, Jillian had sat at the rehearsal dinner and decided to make a change. And she'd made one, a little one, but the effects had been ricocheting crazily through her life ever since. What she had to do now wasn't little and it wasn't easy. But if she wanted anything to be different, she had to do it.

Which meant picking up the phone.

She turned back to her desk. He hadn't called. It had been four days and he hadn't called. Maybe he'd been busy. Maybe he'd been out of town. Maybe he'd already written her off as too much trouble.

And maybe he was waiting for her.

Just do it.

Squaring her shoulders, she picked up the card he'd given her the first day. "I must be nuts," she muttered to herself. It was Thursday. If he'd wanted to see her again, she would have heard from him. How pathetic to call him up when he didn't want her. How much more pathetic to bring him a sad tale of woe.

But she missed him, pure and simple. She'd grown used to his company and life without him was less bright. It didn't matter that he was involved with the paper, she missed the man she'd gotten to know.

And before she could talk herself out of it, she picked up the phone and began to dial.

Gil stared at Fetzer, ignoring his ringing phone. "Robbie Logan's gone?"

"Interesting news, eh? Seems our bright boy didn't just resign from the Children's Connection. He's gone. Disappeared. Into the wind. Whsst." Fetzer made a cutting motion across his neck.

"And no one knows where he's at?"

"No one. Including his probation officer, according to my department mole."

Violating probation. The courts had cut Robbie a deal because he'd helped shut down Charlie Prescott's babynapping ring. If he really had disappeared without notice and the Corrections Department got wind of it, all bets would be off.

Gil shook his head. "I haven't heard a word about this. Who's your source?"

"A department secretary who works ob-gyn at Portland General. Seems she overheard a couple of family members talking last week."

"You're sure on this?"

"I staked out his house yesterday and today. No cars in the driveway until his wife came home. Neighbor guy out cutting his lawn said he hasn't seen him since back in April. According to the court docs, he's supposed to report to his P.O. monthly by phone." Fetzer gave a wolfish smile. "Interesting, no? Makes you wonder where he's gone."

"Where who's gone?" a voice asked, and they saw Russ Gleason in the doorway.

Gil cursed mentally. "Robbie Logan. He seems to be out of town."

"Missing, more like. For at least the last three weeks, as near as I can figure," Fetzer said with relish.

"A missing Logan."

"A missing Logan who's violating probation."

Gleason's eyes gleamed. "That ought to sell a few copies of tomorrow's edition."

"Russ, it's not a story," Gil protested. "If you left town or I left town voluntarily, would it be a story?"

"We're not on probation."

"He could be on vacation, visiting relatives, taking a course. There's any number of reasonable explanations." But none of them good enough to get Gil off the hook.

"It's news," Russ said flatly. "You know as well as I do."

Gil checked his watch. Five-thirty. Getting close to deadline. "Have you talked to the family?" he asked Fetzer.

"Talked to the wife's machine," he replied.

"Then we hold until you reach someone," Gil said.

"We're gonna get scooped," Fetzer protested. "This is news."

"A story like this could wind up getting the guy tossed in the clink if we're not careful," Gil reminded him.

"Not our problem. It's his choice."

"I say run it and print any clarification on Saturday," Gleason said.

"It's my call, Russ." Gil resisted the urge to rub

his temples. He wanted, more than anything, to kill the story, but his only reason for doing so would be his feelings for Jillian.

The two halves of him were at war. One believed that his job was to inform, that there was honor in his work. The other, through Jillian, had begun to see the human cost of what he did. Except that if he didn't run the story simply because of his feelings for the Logans, he'd be betraying readers and the best part of himself.

And if he did run it, he was desperately afraid he'd be losing Jillian forever.

The hell of it was, Fetzer and Gleason were right. The *Gazette* needed to carry the piece. There really wasn't any choice at all.

Gil exhaled slowly and nodded. "All right," he said quietly. "Write the story. If you get confirmation from somewhere, we'll run it. But I don't want speculation and I don't want a witch hunt, Mark. We're not the tabloids. We play it clean."

Fetzer winked. "Just call me Squeaky."

The silence of the office after they'd left seemed incongruous to Gil, given the magnitude of the decision he'd just made. It seemed as though he should have heard the roar of walls tumbling, ceilings falling in.

Instead, his cursor blinked serenely on his computer screen.

He had to call Jillian. He had to tell her. At the very least, he owed her that, and he owed it to himself. Taking a deep breath, Gil picked up the phone and dialed.

"Jillian Logan."

The sound of that calm, cool, measured voice had him squeezing his eyes shut. To think he'd been worried about them before Fetzer had stuck his head in the door. What they'd been up against then was nothing compared to now. He gave a mental curse. "Jillian, it's Gil."

"Gil." He heard pleasure and nerves in equal parts. "You got my message?"

"Message?" he repeated, and realized his voice mail light was blinking. "No, I didn't. I've been in a conference. Listen, we need to talk."

"Yes, we do." No pleasure now, just nerves. "That's what the message was about. I was hoping we could get together tonight, if you're not busy."

"I'm not. When do you want to do it?"

"As soon as you like. I'm leaving now."

"Now works for me," he said, his mouth dry. "Want to meet at my place, say, fifteen minutes?"

"I'll see you then," she said.

He could picture her in her office, cool and tidy. And he hung up the phone with a feeling of doom.

Chapter Thirteen

Jillian rode the elevator up to Gil's floor, watching the numbers light one at a time. She clutched her purse, her palms damp. It was the moment of truth. She just had to walk in and do it.

But what had seemed obvious and straightforward when she'd been talking to Lois was now almost overwhelming as she left the elevator to walk down the hallway and stand before his door.

For a long moment, she just focused on the paint, at the gold and burgundy stripes on the wallpaper beside it. It would be like going off the high dive when she was a kid: easy to contemplate, terrifying when she was up on the board, but over quickly so long as she just made herself start walking and took the leap.

The fatal pause was what would kill her.

Taking a deep breath, she raised her hand and knocked.

He'd been pacing for a good five minutes when the knock came, pacing because he couldn't stand still.

Because he dreaded the discussion to come.

Gil opened the door to see Jillian, dressed in one of her quiet, tidy business suits, a teasing hint of cream-colored lace in the vee of the neckline, her hair twisted up on top of her head. She almost vibrated with tension, strain hovering around the corners of her mouth. After four long days, he ached to touch her but there was too much between them. There were things he had to say.

Instead, he stepped back from the door. "Come on in."

She walked inside, her movements abrupt and too quick. Anxiety rolled off her in waves. "Thanks for making time to get together."

"Happy to do it," he said. It was like they were talking about a business meeting, for Christ's sake, instead of a discussion that could destroy everything. "Can I get you something to drink?"

She shook her head.

"How about a seat, instead?" He went over to the couch and, after a moment, she followed.

And then there was no more excuse to delay. "We need to talk," he began.

"Yes," she said, "we do."

"There's something you should know," he said, but she shook her head.

"Please." Her voice was tight with strain. "Let me go first."

"Jillian, I have to tell you something."

Her attempt at a smile didn't quite make it. "Shh." She put her fingertips against his lips. He could feel her trembling. "Please?"

"But—"

"There are things I need to tell you, too, and if I don't start, I'm going to lose my nerve. Just let me talk." Her eyes pleaded with him. "Afterward, you can say whatever you like."

Like had nothing to do with it. It was honor, pure and simple. But with her gazing at him in entreaty, looking as though she was holding herself together with pure nerve, what could he do but say yes? And helplessly, he nodded.

Jillian took a deep breath. "Things got a little strange the other night. And you asked me about what happened but I just wasn't…" She shook her head. "I wasn't in a place where I could talk about it. It's funny. I counsel people all day about dealing with their feelings and their pasts, but when it comes to me—" she lifted her shoulder "—I don't always do so well."

"Sometimes it's easier to keep the world at a distance."

"Maybe. But you're not the world. You said something to me Saturday night, about us. You said that it mattered to you, what we're doing here. It matters to me, too. And talking to you about this—talking to anyone—scares the hell out of me but I want to do it. For you, and for me."

"Jillian—"

"Just please, let me talk," she whispered. It was the prelude but it wasn't what she needed to tell him. It was the reason but not the story. The hardest part still lay ahead. Gil subsided, waiting quietly, watching her.

"The other night—" she began, and moistened her lips. "The other night—" she said again.

And she was back on the high dive, staring down helplessly at the water. She hadn't known to just walk without thinking that first time. She'd climbed the ladder, anxiety growing with every rung she passed. Then at the end of the board, she'd stood and stared down at the water with roiling stomach, fear choking her, fear of jumping, fear of turning back.

The same way fear choked her now.

Gil reached over and took her hand. "Talk to me," he said softly.

She knew she needed to do it but it was so hard, so hard. She took a breath, concentrating on the warmth of his fingers around hers. "You may have noticed that I'm not the most...experienced woman in the world. I haven't been with a lot of men. Any men," she corrected, staring down at their linked hands, unable to bear seeing shock, disbelief, pity appear in his eyes. "I've kissed but I've never had... I never—" She swallowed and forced out the words. "I'm a virgin."

"All of us were at one time or another."

His voice was quiet, calm. She gave him a startled glance to find his expression unsurprised. "Not at thirty-three."

"So you're a late bloomer," he said. "It's not a big deal. The reason why is. With your looks, I imagine you've had more than your share of opportunities."

"Not as many as you'd think."

"A choice. You're good at keeping people away. Except for maybe pushy guys like me."

She found herself smiling. "Except for pushy guys like you," she agreed, and squeezed his fingers. It was easier to talk touching him, watching the sky beyond the windows turn ruddy with the light of the setting sun.

"So what is the why?" he asked.

She moved her shoulders. "I've never known. There have been a couple of times with guys that things started to go beyond a kiss—college, my midtwenties—and it was like what happened with us. One minute I'd be feeling good, the next I'd just panic. It was like something else took over my body. I never understood why and the guys—" she hesitated "—the guys never had much patience with it."

"I figured something was up when you just shut down."

"It wasn't you. What we did felt amazing. It was so good I thought maybe I would finally be okay, maybe I could… But I freaked, the same way I always do." And she'd been sure that the relationship was done, the same way it always had been before, leaving her to retreat to her burrow like a small, wounded animal.

"Have you ever talked with someone about it?"

She gave a humorless smile. "I'm a licensed social worker. That's what we do. I've had years of therapy."

"And?"

Now they'd come down to it, the hard part. She took a deep breath. "I didn't have what you'd call a regular childhood."

"Were you abused?"

Jillian hesitated. *Just do it*. But she couldn't

quite go there yet. "Not sexually," she compromised. "That's been part of the problem. It's hard to fix something emotionally when you don't know what it is."

"And you know now?"

She nodded slowly. "I think so. Lois helped me understand. I saw something when I was very young, a...couple having rough sex. I don't remember many other details except that she was crying out."

"How old were you?"

"Three, maybe four."

"Pretty intense for a small child."

What kind of miracle was it that he understood? "I didn't know what they were doing. And when you're a child and you see something you don't comprehend, you frame it in terms of things you do. I thought he was attacking her. And so now I panic."

Gil put his fingertips to her chin, turned her head so that she was looking at him. "I wouldn't ever hurt you intentionally, Jillian," he said quietly. "Do you believe that?"

She put her hand to his cheek. "Yes," she whispered. "I don't believe you'd intentionally hurt anyone."

"So what happens now?"

"Understanding it means being able to deal

with it. Maybe knowing why I panic now means I can try to make myself release and get past it." She swallowed. "I've told you because I don't want it to end with what happened the other night. I'm tired of this. I want more."

"There is more."

"I want to know what it's like." She summoned up every bit of courage she possessed and pressed her mouth to his, sliding her fingers up through his hair. "Make love with me, Gil," she whispered against his lips. "I want to know."

"Ah, Jillian," he said huskily. "I need to tell—"

She stopped his words with a kiss. "Later," she said, praying he'd agree because she didn't know how much longer she could keep up the bravado. "Please?"

He surprised her by sighing. "I really think we should wait until you're not so upset."

"I'm not upset anymore." Even she could hear the trembling in her voice. She unbuttoned her jacket to show the silk-and-lace camisole beneath.

"Jillian, I'm serious. This isn't the time."

"Yes, it is." It had to be. She didn't know that she would ever find the nerve again. "I need this, Gil. Are you going to make me beg?" She took a breath, prayed for courage and pressed his hand to her breast.

He let out an explosive breath. His fingers

twitched against her for an instant. And then he was taking her by the shoulders and moving her away. "No, okay?" he said roughly, and rubbed a hand against his forehead. "Give me a break. There's only so much I can stand."

It was like having ice poured over her. She felt herself shrinking in the sudden blast of cold.

There's only so much I can stand.

He didn't want her. How had she gotten it so wrong? Somehow, she'd miscalculated. Somehow, she'd misread the signs. She'd been turned on, he'd been waiting for it to be over. She'd been ready to go to bed with him, he'd just been patronizing the basket case. All the while, she could still feel the heat of his hand on her breast. She wanted to disappear into the cushions.

Instead, she rose. "Okay, well, so much for that." Her voice was brisk. "I should get going."

"What?" He gave her an incredulous stare as she moved to get her purse. "Wait a minute, you're not going anywhere."

"Yes, I am. You've been very nice but I've taken enough of your time." She didn't want to look at him because she had the horrible feeling she would cry. The door, she thought. The door was only a few steps away. If she could get on the other side of it, she'd be okay.

And then she heard two quick steps behind her

and he was spinning her around to pull her into his arms and fuse his mouth to hers.

It took her hard and deep, dizzying her for a moment, until she leaned away. "Gil, you don't have to do this. It's okay if you don't want me."

"Are you out of your mind?" His eyes narrowed and he pulled her to him again. Heat bloomed, as it always did, the arousal billowing up within her. There was nothing of politeness in the kiss. There was an urgency, a demand that coursed from his body into hers until it ignited desire.

He kissed his way over her cheeks, along her jaw, down to her throat. Her purse thudded to the floor. "God, you're so sexy," he muttered against her skin. "How could you think I wouldn't want you? I've wanted you since I laid eyes on you. And we are going to do this. Now."

He took her by the hand and led her to the stairs.

His bedroom was clean-lined and masculine, with black cabinets and a pewter-colored coverlet pulled down to reveal snowy-white sheets. The lamps were of some dull silvery metal. At the end of the loft, the railing looked out over the living room below.

The nerves had returned in the time it had taken to mount the stairs. Jillian'd been sure of what she wanted when she'd set things in motion, but now, with time to think, anxiety was rising up to swamp the desire. What if she couldn't get past it and relax? What if she panicked again?

What if she couldn't please him?

As though he sensed her tension, Gil turned and pulled her to him for a long kiss. "Relax," he murmured. "We've got all the time in the world." He reached to the wall to snap a switch and a soft nimbus of light began to glow around the perimeter of the room.

"You want the lights on?" she asked unevenly.

"Just a little. I want to see you." He eased her jacket off her shoulders. "You have no idea how much these suits drive me crazy. They look so demure but then you have this lace showing at the neckline and all I want to do is find out what's underneath." He unclipped her hair and plunged his hands into the heavy mass of it. Then he was walking her backward until she could feel the bed against her legs, easing her down onto the coverlet.

For a moment, he looked at her, clad in her silk-and-lace camisole and trousers. "This is real, right? I'm not dreaming this?" Jillian felt the mattress give as he moved onto the bed beside her and leaned over her to press his lips to hers. "Your mouth makes me nuts," he muttered. "It did from the first time I saw you, out on the street. I look at that bottom lip of yours and I just want it."

When he kissed her this time, it was with an

urgency and demand that sent a thrill spiraling through her. She felt the silk of her camisole slide against her skin as his hand slipped down her back, over her waist, making her shiver, making goose bumps rise. With a groan, he pressed his lips to her throat.

He explored, roving along the smooth column, lingering over the hollow at the base. Jillian slipped her arms around him as he licked his way over the fragile skin of her chest and down lower, until he met the silk and lace of her camisole.

This time when his hand moved up her torso, he grazed her with the back of his hand, running his knuckles up over her silk-covered stomach, over her breast. She caught her breath at the feel of it, her open mouth resting against his own, their heads side by side on the pillow. Then his fingers worked their way under the silk to stroke the bare skin of her belly.

It sent a shiver through her. For a breathless instant his fingers danced over her fabric-covered breasts. And it was maddening, suddenly, to feel only a muted echo of his touch, separated from where she ached for him by the fabric of her bra.

She made an impatient noise, and he laughed softly. "Sounds like we need to get this out of the way."

He slipped his hands under the camisole and

began pulling it up. For an instant, she tensed, and he pressed his mouth back over hers, persuading her with lips and tongue, making her forget self-consciousness in the rush of pleasure.

"You're so gorgeous," he whispered as he eased it off, "so hot. I want to see you."

She lay with her arms still curved up over her head. Gil moved to whip off his shirt, then sank back down beside her, reaching out to trace his fingertips down her throat, over her collarbones and along the slant of her chest. Nerve by nerve, her body came to thrumming alert. He ran his fingers around the edges of her bra, his touch on her bare skin only making her want more.

Closing her eyes, Jillian let the mix of sensations flow over her as he kissed her, caressed her, loved her.

This time, when he traced his fingers down her body again, she twisted against him, dragging him close for an impatient, needy kiss.

"I guess you want this off," he said, unsnapping the front clasp of her bra and peeling back first one cup, then another. And, before she could tense, he slipped his hand up over her bare breast in a move of almost shocking intimacy.

Sensation whipped through her, wrenching a gasp from her throat. The wave of pleasure was exquisite. His palm was hard and hot against her sensitive skin. When he squeezed, she twisted against him, making an incoherent noise.

Then he leaned over to press a kiss on her lips, laying his upper body atop hers.

The feel of his naked chest against her own was exquisite, a warm intimacy, a startling immediacy. Self-consciousness was forgotten in the sheer fascination of the touch.

Then he began to rove again, not with his hands, this time but his mouth. He brushed his lips down over the thin skin at the top of her breasts and her nipples tingled with want. He circled the tip of his tongue around the areola of first one breast, then the other, until she was quivering with suppressed excitement. He kept tracing the warm, wet trail inward and farther inward until she was arching toward him.

Then suddenly he put his open mouth on the sensitive peak.

Jillian cried out and bucked against him. It was like nothing she'd ever felt before. His mouth was hot and determined. His tongue swirled against her, sending bursts of pleasure through her. And though his mouth was touching only there, she felt the answering tug below.

She was a delight, a wonder, Gil thought as she quivered beneath his hands. He'd never been with a woman so sensitive. He'd never been a woman's first time. Seeing her respond to his caresses was incredibly arousing. Seeing her reaction to each new sensation had him fighting to maintain control. He wanted to show her everything. He wanted to make it magic. He wanted it to last forever.

He didn't know whether this would be the last and only time.

He schooled himself to go slow, even though the need pounded through him. He was so hard he was aching as he slid his hand down over her satiny torso. Every movement she made, every sound of pleasure pulled him closer to the edge.

His hand strayed to the button of her trousers. "I think we're done with these for now," he murmured, unzipping them to find his way under the silk and lace she wore beneath. Startled, she caught her breath.

The heat, the arousal intensified with the feel of his hand and she moaned a little. It felt too good, too intense, until her entire consciousness was focused on that spot, that one burning spot where he touched her. Then he moved lower and slipped a fingertip inside her.

And the panic hit. She tensed, her breath coming shallow. Arousal disappeared, washed away by the flood of anxiety.

Gil moved his hand, pulled her tight to him. "It's okay," he whispered. "Trust me."

"I'm sorry," she said, rolling away from him, fighting tears.

"We have all the time in the world," he said, pressing kisses to her shoulders and her neck, slipping his arms around her. Slowly, she began to relax.

He began pulling down her trousers, inch by inch, stroking the exposed skin. Jillian could feel the cool air of the room. She felt the fabric slide against her thighs.

Felt him hook his fingers around the silk at her hips and drag it down.

And then she was naked.

Chapter Fourteen

Jillian fought the urge to cover herself. Being naked in front of a man required a level of vulnerability that had always seemed unimaginable. This wasn't just any man, though. This was Gil, and it would be okay.

Then Gil moved up over the end of the bed and began licking his way up her thighs and the slow beat of desire began within her again. Warm, wet kisses, the sudden surprising slide of his tongue. She'd never known that her skin could be so sensitive. He kept at it, moving upward until she was mindless, unaware of the moans she made, her hips moving rhythmically against his touch. She began to tremble.

And then his mouth was on her, sudden and hot and her body arched up off the bed in shock. Nothing had prepared her for this. No touch of her hands had prepared her for the wet heat, the maddeningly slick strokes, the utterly unpredictable caresses that drove her relentlessly upward.

His clever mouth did things to her that she'd never even imagined until she was a creature of pure sensation, existing only for the pleasure, the coiling intensity of want that tightened and tightened until all of her, every atom of her was focused on that one spot, that one burning spot that he was tormenting with the hot, wet heat of his tongue.

Her hands fisted on the sheets. She rolled her head from side to side, moaning, gasping, clenching.

And suddenly, like a revelation, the orgasm exploded through her. Blasts of sensation rushed throughout her entire body to the tips of her fingers and toes as she shook and jolted and cried out helplessly. It was nearly overwhelming and it lasted a long time, finally subsiding into a warm glow, punctuated by the occasional quakes of the aftershocks.

Gil moved up the bed to lie alongside her.

"Oh," she half gasped, half laughed. "Oh, my."

"I take it that means that you liked it?"

She rolled him on his back and kissed him exuberantly. "That was the most amazing thing

I've ever felt. You should get a public monument made to you."

"A public monument? The mind boggles," he said.

"Maybe something a little more private."

"Private works. And while we're talking about private…"

There was a little note of strain in his voice. There was still more to come, she realized. And there was his release. "I guess we should do something for you, shouldn't we?"

"Are you kidding? This has all been for me."

For the first time, she registered the hard mass against her hip.

"Do you want to keep going?" he asked softly.

When she nodded, he rose up off the bed to shuck his shoes and jeans and shorts.

She knew what to expect, of course. She'd read books. Nothing had prepared her for the sight of his arousal, though. It rose from his body, thick and powerful. She stared at it, mesmerized, as he slid back onto the bed.

"I want you, Jillian," he murmured.

She reached out tentatively and traced her fingertips down his belly. Gil's breath hissed in and the muscles of his belly tightened into fascinating bricks. Emboldened, she drew her fingers down lower, to where the trail of dark hair started. "I don't know what to do," she whispered.

"You're doing fine," he said, his voice strained.

She bit her lip in concentration, staring at him. Curiosity warred with nerves and won. And she reached for him. Shock, arousal, surprise. Amazement. Who knew that a man's body could have something so smooth yet startlingly solid, like silk over granite?

Gil groaned. Need began to build in Jillian again. She could give him pleasure, not just take it. It was a heady feeling.

Swiftly, Gil fused his mouth to hers. This wasn't lazy seduction any more but hard urgency, naked demand. He bit at her lips, took the kiss deep as she caressed him. The tension, the scent of arousal rose.

And then he made a noise of impatience. This was it, she thought as he pressed her onto her back. Amid the wanting was a flutter of nerves but mostly she felt impatience. She wanted to unveil the mystery. She wanted to know. She wanted it all.

Gil moved between her legs. The feel of his bare skin against her entire body was outrageously erotic, extravagantly seductive. Jillian stared up into his eyes. They were so black, so intense that they felt like inky pools that spread out to encompass her, to encompass her world. Nothing else mattered. All that mattered was here, this moment, this man.

And then she jolted and gasped as she felt him rub the velvety soft tip of himself through the slick folds between her legs.

It was happening, she realized. She fought to take in a breath with lungs that felt robbed of oxygen. Her heart hammered as if it was trying to batter its way out of her chest.

Gil's face was drawn taut with the effort of control. He poised himself at her entrance, she could feel it with nerves that were hypersensitive. When he eased himself inside a fraction, she tightened her fingers on his back. All of her was focused on that spot as he moved in just another fraction of an inch. Then he stopped. Jillian felt a pressure inside her. She knew that this was it.

He slipped his hand between them and stroked her, making her shiver. The sharp, immediate surface thrill of his caresses on the hard bud of her sex was somehow dwarfed by the sensation of him partly inside her. He was moving just a little, in and out of her entrance, rubbing her, teasing her, maddening her, making her wait in unbearable tension.

"Please," she gasped.

And with a quick pump of his hips, he was inside her. Her breath hissed in at the quick, slicing pain and the surprising sensation of being completely filled.

"Are you all right?" he ground out.

They were twined together, connected utterly. It was extraordinary, the heat, the intimacy of being so completely fused with another. Jillian could feel him everywhere around her, on her, within her. "Better than all right," she said breathlessly.

Some instinct had her raising her hips to meet his. Some instinct had her raising her legs to wrap around him to bring him closer. "Show me," she whispered.

And he began to stroke.

He was slow and careful at first, moving the hard length of himself in and out of her. And the pain disappeared, replaced by a gradually growing excitement. Each stroke caressed her inside and out. Each stroke, her arousal built afresh.

And each slow, powerful thrust made her shiver with a deeper arousal than she'd ever felt before, a thrumming intensity that had her transfixed. Gradually, his cadence increased. Gradually, his breath came faster. Jillian clasped her hands against his back, feeling the slippery bunch and flow of his muscles, feeling the weight of him against her, feeling the rhythm of his thrusts. And all the sensations melded into one, an almost overwhelming mix that had her gasping. She didn't think she could stand it. She didn't think her body could encompass so much pleasure without simply burning up. She stared up into his face, his beautiful face, drawn tight and pure as he watched her, waiting for her as he dragged her closer and closer and closer to the ultimate release.

And then she was climaxing as abruptly as if she'd been flung over some invisible edge, crying out and jolting against him for long, endless, shuddering minutes.

Even as she quaked, Gil stroked once, twice, three times and then he was groaning and spilling himself into her as she still clenched around him.

He'd move, Gil thought. In a moment he'd move, as soon as he got over being stunned from what surely had to be the most cataclysmic sex of his entire life. He sucked in a breath and raised himself up enough to roll off and lie beside her.

Jillian lay against him, not moving.

"Are you okay?" he asked. She hadn't seemed to react much to the pain so much as pleasure, but maybe he'd been wrong. He wanted it to have been good for her. Hell, forget good, he wanted it to have been amazing. Her life had changed profoundly in the past hour.

And maybe his had, as well.

Jillian made a throaty, satisfied sound. "I'm fabulous. I had absolutely no idea." She turned to her side and traced a pattern on his chest with her fingertip. "Is it always like that?"

"Like that? I can pretty confidently say no." He'd had sex plenty of times. But he'd never had those moments of complete mental and physical connection. They'd become one in more than just the physical sense. When he'd climaxed, he'd felt as though some part of his soul was pouring into her at the same time.

And in that moment, everything had changed. Or, rather, all the changes that had been happening since he'd met her had piled up, one on another, coalescing into one shivering, blinding revelation: he was in love with her.

She gave him an amused look. "Are you all right?"

"Who, me? Yeah." Outside of the fact that the pieces of his world had just realigned themselves in a new and startling pattern, sure.

"You just had an odd look on your face."

It was a bit of an odd feeling. But not bad, he realized. Actually, it felt pretty damned good. He pulled her close for a kiss. "You're amazing."

She looked at him for a long moment. "Thank you," she said quietly.

"It's just the truth."

"No. I mean, thank you for this. For showing me what it was about."

He snorted. "It wasn't a charity effort, Jillian. I did it because I wanted you and I enjoyed every minute of it."

"But you were kind and patient. You made it good for me. Better than good. Incredible. I'd never imagined it could be like that." She gave him an impish smile. "Although, I'm pretty sure there are a few other aspects of the process that we could explore."

"Now? Come on, woman, give me a couple of hours at least. I'm thirty-eight, not eighteen."

She rolled over to prop herself on his chest. "I suppose if we can't have sex again yet, lying together naked is a close second."

He slid his hands down her back and over the rise of her ass. "There's a lot to be said for lying together naked."

"I think you're right." She sighed. "And in the meantime, since you're such an old, decrepit specimen, you can tell me whatever it was you wanted to say earlier. Unless present activities took care of it."

And all the lazy happiness went away. This was the moment he'd dreaded, the moment he'd known was coming. And now he had to figure out how to handle it, now that he was in deeper than ever.

"There's something you should know about."

"I think you just got done showing me what I

really needed to know." She kissed him, her mouth open and warm and eager enough that he felt himself starting to harden.

"No," he said edgily. "This is important."

Slowly, subtly, she came to attention. "What's important?"

"It's the *Gazette,* tomorrow's edition."

She moved away from him then, pulling the sheet around her, her eyes huge and dark.

"We're running a story." He took a breath. "On Robbie."

And her face went sheet-white. "On Robbie?" Her voice was barely audible.

"One of our reporters says he's disappeared. The reporter is getting final confirmation. It'll run tomorrow."

"You're running a story that he's disappeared?" Her voice sounded as though she'd swallowed razor blades.

And in her eyes, he saw the answer.

"It's true, isn't it?"

"That's none of your business," she said sharply.

"Where is he, Jillian?"

"Don't you dare pump me," she hissed.

"If he doesn't get back, the law will come down on him like a ton of bricks."

"Don't you think we know that?" she snapped. "We've been doing everything we could to get him back. And now you're going to blow it all out of the water so you can sell a few thousand extra papers."

"Unfortunately, it's news. If he hadn't run, there'd have been nothing to print."

"Let me get this straight. We live in a city of a million and a half people and you're telling me the only thing you could put in your paper is a story that's going to destroy my family?"

"It's not aimed at you. Don't make this about us." He reached out to touch her cheek but she jerked away from him, rising off the bed and dragging the sheet with her.

"You're running a story that's going to tell the entire world, including his P.O., that my brother's violated his probation, which will very likely get him thrown in jail, and you're trying to tell me it has nothing to do with *us?*" Her voice rose in incredulous fury.

"Don't do this, Jillian," Gil pleaded. "It tore me up to give the okay because I knew how you'd feel, but I had to. At least, this way I can control the shape of it, make sure it's as accurate as possible."

"Is that supposed to make me feel better? 'Jillian, I'd never intentionally hurt you,'" she mocked savagely, picking her clothing up garment by garment. "My *God.*"

He whitened as though she'd slapped him. "We're Portland's biggest daily. When something happens in the community, we have to cover it. That's what we do."

"No you don't." Her voice was ripe with contempt. "What you do is make money by tearing people's lives apart."

The betrayal sliced through her like a knife. She'd opened herself to him utterly in the most fundamental of ways and all the while he'd carried the explosive secret of the damning story. And now she was here, naked, her clothes strewn all around the room, her body still smelling of his.

Her throat closed up.

"It would have wound up in the paper sooner or later," he said quietly. "If nothing else, we always publish the crime sheet. He shouldn't have run."

"He ran because the media was hounding him to death." She struggled to pull on her underwear beneath the sheet, wishing to God she didn't feel so hideously exposed. "Your newspaper started it, dredging up the past for no reason. You keep telling me it's about the news. That wasn't news. It wasn't fraud in the new streetcar line, it wasn't pollution. It's one man's life. Since when did that become public property?"

"When the man in question has gone from helping kidnap children to running a day care center," Gil retorted, dragging on his jeans. "You couldn't possibly think that it wasn't going to cause a scandal when people heard."

"Why didn't you get our side? Why did you use the most condemning quotes from every city and state politician you could find, from psychologists who knew nothing about the case? They had a political ax to grind and you let them use Robbie to grind it." Impatiently, she dropped the sheet. It didn't matter if she was exposed and humiliated. She'd already been stripped as naked as she could be. "He was making a new life. He was building something and you took him down."

"What about the parents who didn't know and accept Robbie's past? It was in the public's interest that it be reported."

"And you know as well as I do that things can be slanted by the choice of an adjective. And brother, did they get slanted." She pulled her camisole on.

"We can't control what the tabloids and the TV stations do."

"No, you just shout 'fire' in a crowded room and walk out." She dragged on her trousers and buttoned them. "You can't keep pretending that the subjects of your stories aren't people, Gil. You have to take responsibility."

"Responsibility? Can you honestly tell me that if this weren't your family, if you didn't work at the Children's Connection, you'd think a baby kidnapper running a day care center was fine?" he challenged.

"If he were the monster that the papers made him out to be, yes. But he's not, he's a human being trying his best to do the right thing."

"Including violating probation?"

She ignored him. "When does a man get a chance to redeem himself? When does he get to be taken on the strength of the present, not the past? The police got Charlie Prescott because of Robbie. He'd tried to fix the damage. But you don't care about that, do you? All you care about is selling newspapers."

She saw the fury leap into his eyes. "I don't give a damn about selling newspapers. I care about telling the truth. I care about serving this community. And the only thing that made me think twice about this story was knowing what it would do to you. If it had been any other person, I'd have run it in a heartbeat." He dragged his hands through his hair. "I have an obligation as an editor to see that the paper reports the news, Jillian. I can't let the fact that I'm involved with you cloud that."

"*Involved* with me?" she repeated incredulously. "Are you out of your mind? After all this, you think we're involved? You can't separate one from the other. You can't attack my people, my life and say it's your sacred profession and it shouldn't bother me." She snatched up her jacket and turned to the stairs.

"And if I put aside my ethics, violate my principles and pull the story to protect Robbie, that would be okay?" he demanded, hot on her heels. "It's a public trust, Jillian."

"It's too bad you're too busy worrying about your public trust you can't take care of personal trust," she hurled back.

"What do you know about personal trust? All you've done from the beginning is block me out."

"Block you out?" She turned at the bottom of the stairs. "How can you say that?"

"Because of tonight? Oh, sure, you opened up a little but you didn't tell me everything, not even a fraction. Do you think I don't see those mile-high walls when they go up? Everything I've ever gotten from you I've had to fight you tooth and nail for. Except tonight."

"And look what I got in return," she flung back at him. "I'm so *glad* I opened up to you. I mean, if you were going to screw me, you might as well do it all the way."

"Jesus." The word exploded out of him. "What happened here tonight was one of the most amazing experiences in my life. Don't you for one minute try to turn it into something else. We connected, you and I, and if it weren't for the outside world, everything would have all been great. But we live in the outside world and we live with your family and my paper and this god-damned, stupid conflict. And I am not going to turn myself into someone neither of us can respect to protect your lawbreaking brother."

"That's right, you have a public trust." She headed for the door.

"Don't start with the trust thing. You've never trusted me once since this whole thing began."

"For good reason."

"Not for good reason. Because you're scared. Because something happened to you a long time ago and instead of having the guts to face it and get past it, you'd rather hide away from the whole world. That's not what relationships are supposed to be about," he raged. "And you, of all people, should know that."

"You're upset that I wouldn't open up? That I wouldn't tell you about my childhood?" She rounded on him. "What do you want to hear? That I'm not really a Logan? That my real mother was a crackhead? That she was the one I saw having bondage sex with a boyfriend? Or maybe a john. It's hard to know when you're only three or four." She delivered the lines as though they were blows, heedless in her fury. "We lived in filthy rat holes, Gil. When she needed to go score drugs, she'd lock us up and sometimes forget to let us out for days. And then she got tired of it and dumped us on my grandmother, except *she'd* had a stroke and couldn't speak. We had to work out our own language. We barely spoke English. And she kept having ministrokes, as near as I can tell, because after a while she couldn't even take care of herself, let alone us, so we were starving and running around filthy, like animals.

"We were freaks, Gil." Tears began to slip down her cheeks. "Is that what you wanted to hear? Is that what you need for your profile?"

"God, Jillian," he said helplessly. "I didn't know."

And she turned away so that she wouldn't have to see the one thing she couldn't bear from him.

Pity.

Escape, she thought, focusing on the door. She had to get out.

"Wait a minute," Gil said. "You can't walk away now, not after that."

"Oh, yes, I can. You just watch me." She snatched up her purse.

"You don't have to keep doing this alone, Jillian. Remember what you told Alison? You've got people who care about you. I care about you."

She wasn't going to listen, wasn't going to let herself feel. "You? The guy who's running a smear campaign on my brother?"

"No. The guy who's fallen in love with you."

The words rang in the sudden silence. "No—" she shook her head blindly "—that's not fair, Gil. Don't play games with me."

"I'm not. Don't go, Jillian. It doesn't have to be like this. We can make it work."

"We can't, don't you see?" She turned to him, eyes filled with despair. "Not here, not now. One of us has to lose. It can't be you, you tell me." She put her hand on the doorknob. "And I've already lost too much. Goodbye, Gil."

And she made herself walk out the door.

Chapter Fifteen

It was a shock to walk out of Gil's building and still see the light of late afternoon. Impossible that it could still be the same day. How could she have gone from absolute bliss to utter despair in such a short time? How could everything that mattered in her life have crumbled? Even her body didn't feel right as she walked along the street, jerky, disjointed as though she was some kind of windup toy that had been battered and bent.

She shook her head, trying to come out of her daze. She had to call her family, call Nancy and warn them. She dug her cell phone out of her purse. But just as the call started to connect, her throat tightened and she began to shake.

She pressed the End button and waited for composure. She just needed a couple of minutes and then she would call. But the shaking didn't go away. It didn't go away as she walked to the bus stop; it didn't go away as she waited for her ride. And it didn't go away as she text messaged David because she'd realized, finally, that it wasn't going to go away, not for a long, long while.

So she rode the bus home, grateful for the unspoken compact that the commuters crammed cheek by jowl would look through one another. She put on sunglasses and sat by the window, staring out as clouds swept in to mask the setting sun. And if she wept behind the dark lenses, no one commented.

Gil sat at his desk, looking out the window at the giant blue ribbons that ran along the sides of the Portland Building. A honk from a car in the street outside made him start and blink. He'd been staring into space again, he thought, shaking his head. He'd been doing that a lot over the past few days. Something about having life go to hell in a handbasket overnight—hell, in a matter of hours—tended to do that to a person.

Of course, he supposed it didn't matter all that much if he stared into space a little, considering it was a Saturday. He'd come in do a final review of Jillian's profile, which was set to run the next day. Although he was kidding himself. The article was in the can, had been long since.

But it was a way to avoid his condo, which echoed with her angry words, and his boat, which still resonated with her laughter. It was a way to avoid the memories of her that hovered all around him. Too many for such a short time. And how was it they were lodged everywhere, ready to ambush him at every turn?

Impatient with himself, he pulled over a manila folder his copy editor had tossed down on his desk. "Needs cutline," read the sticky note on top.

And he opened the folder, only to see Jillian staring up at him. It was a picture of her sitting in the chair in her office, legs crossed, a swing of dark hair framing her face. The photographer had managed to capture her in the attitude of listening, concentrating with her eyes, her face, her whole body. For an instant, she was all but present in the room.

And the sudden ache for her surged through him.

Why couldn't she understand that pulling a story for personal reasons was against every principle of journalism he'd ever learned? It wasn't as simple as protecting Robbie or protecting her. It wasn't even as simple as violating who he was. It was bigger than that. The ripples spread out into the world, to every person who picked up the paper because they thought it was telling them how the shape of their community had changed that day.

Not that it was telling them what was convenient for the personal life of the editor. Why couldn't she see that?

Because it hurt her, he thought immediately. Because she felt an obligation, a compulsion to save Robbie, to see that he was protected.

The way she hadn't been.

It sliced through him, the thought of what had happened to her as a child. He'd known she had secrets, but nothing like this. He ached for her. He ached over the fact that he hadn't known. Why hadn't she opened up to him? Why hadn't she let him help? Instead, she'd kept it all locked inside, then wielded it as a weapon.

They could be so much together, he thought in impotent frustration. But he was kidding himself. How did you build a relationship with someone who blocked you out? How did you get to know someone when they kept the walls up all around them?

What haunted him, though, was the end of it all, her expression desperate and shattered, her voice vibrating with remembered pain. All he could do was feel for her.

Damn Robbie Logan for starting the whole mess, he thought in sudden frustration. If he hadn't screwed up, there would have been time to gain Jillian's trust; there would have been time to go slowly, persuade her to reveal her secrets. Instead, the issue of Robbie had catalyzed their differences.

Over the years, Gil had been involved with any number of women. The relationships always ended, usually around the time they started wanting something more from him. In none of those cases had there been the least overlap between his work and their lives. He'd been free to commit if he'd wanted to; he just hadn't wanted to.

And now he'd found the woman who was right for him, the woman he'd connected with, the one with whom he'd clicked. Except that his work and her family had mixed like water and concrete to create a barrier so solid and so high it was impossible to get around.

Damn Robbie Logan, anyway.

And Jillian's voice sounded in his head. *He was making a new life. He was building something and you took him down.*

Like hell, Gil thought. He'd edited those stories. They'd been multisourced. Granted, the first one, the one that had gotten all the play, hadn't had comment from the Logan camp, but they hadn't been slanted.

Had they?

Shaking it off, he turned his attention back to

the photograph and banged out a hasty cutline for his copy editor and sent it.

When does a man get a chance to redeem himself? When does he get to be taken on the strength of the present, not the past?

They'd covered the news, he thought, staring at Jillian's eyes in the photograph. They'd done their job. Restlessly, he drummed his fingers on the desk.

And without even quite deciding to do it, he found himself searching out one Robbie Logan story after another on the *Gazette* Web site. Settling back, he began to read.

Two hours later, he rubbed his chin thoughtfully. The stories hadn't changed since he'd first reviewed them and yet somehow they looked different. *Read* different. Sure, they'd covered the who, what, when, where, why and how, but they hadn't shown the people involved. They hadn't said anything at all about the bigger issues or the mitigating circumstances. Things look different depending on where you're sitting, he'd once told Jillian.

And, boy, they sure looked different now.

Quick and sure, he reached for his keyboard and began to type.

Jillian sat out in her garden, tying up her clematis onto their trellises. She'd waited too long with some of them, she thought, carefully unwinding the curving tendrils that had seized onto the stems of neighboring plants.

"Let go," she gritted as she unwound one. That was the danger. It was always harder to let go when you latched on too quickly to something. Or someone, said a little voice in her head. Like Gil Reynolds. She'd thought she was so smart, keeping him at arm's length, keeping him out, never realizing all the while that he was sneaking under her guard. And while he'd been sneaking under her guard, he'd sneaked into her heart.

No, she thought immediately, not into her heart because that would mean she was in love with him and that would be pure idiocy. Ridiculous. Impossible. So what if she found herself missing him with an almost physical ache? It didn't matter. What mattered was that he'd sabotaged Robbie. He'd sabotaged Robbie and thought it was just fine. And he'd had the gall to blame her for not understanding, attack her for not opening up to him.

Trust issues? Hell, yeah, she had trust issues with the likes of him. He'd had sex with her, taken her virginity, knowing the whole time that the story on Robbie's disappearance was going to run in the *Gazette*. Knowing what it would do to her. Yes, she bore some responsibility for pushing him to go ahead. She still couldn't stop the anger. He'd never apologized, he'd only defended.

And accused her of holding out on him.

The anger flickered through her. What the hell business was it of his, the painful, humiliating details of her past? Why did he have to pry? What right did he have to find out her secrets, to crawl inside her mind?

Because he could help, a voice inside her whispered. And that quickly, she remembered talking to him on the couch, feeling the warmth of his hand holding hers, the acceptance, being held in the safety of his arms.

But he'd betrayed her. And she'd walked away from the betrayal because she'd had to, because there were no easy answers. She'd walked away knowing she might never find that particular feeling again.

Loss boiled up, threatening to overwhelm her. She squeezed her eyes shut. Focus on the anger, she told herself for a whirling moment, clenching her fingers into the earth. Focusing on the anger would let her avoid the things she didn't want to think about. And as the minutes crawled by, she felt the urge to scream ebb away. She opened her eyes and dusted off her hands. The anger would get her through that minute and the next. And the next. And eventually, the feelings would fade away and she'd be able to wake without dreading the day ahead.

* * *

"I have some birth parent letters to show you," Jillian said, two days later to Alison. "Remember, this is just to give you an idea of your options. This isn't to pressure you into any decisions, okay?"

"Okay."

"Now, this one's from John and Anne Sternwood." She handed the document over.

The girl read, frowning a little as she read.

"I know they sound stiff," Jillian said apologetically. "They really are nice people, though. They're committed to providing a good, stable home. You'd be able to meet them, of course, draw your own conclusions. And you'll see they've indicated that they're open to sending a yearly letter and photo to the mother of their child."

Alison nodded, clearly unconvinced. "I just want the baby to be happy," she whispered.

Jillian nodded. "I know. Try this one. It's the birth parent letter for Doug and Shelly Dolan."

"A letter?" Alison took the padded binder. "It looks more like a scrapbook."

"That's Doug and Shelly. They don't do things the way you'd expect but they're good people. It's important to them that you understand who they are and what they're about," Jillian said.

But Alison was already paging through the book, laughing delightedly at the photo of Doug covered in soapsuds, washing the car with one of his young nephews.

"We found each other late," she read off the page.

"That meant both of us had gone through tough times and disappointments. It took us a long time to trust that what we had between us was real but it is and it's lasted. That's why we want so much to share our lives with a child, or hopefully two or three.

"And it doesn't matter if that child is ours biologically or ours as a gift. We have love and a home. Now, we want to fill it with family."

Alison was silent for a moment. When she looked at Jillian, tears shimmered in her eyes. "This is them," she said shakily. "These are the parents for my child."

"You need to meet them," Jillian said. "Make sure you're sure."

"I will and I am," Alison said. "The people who made this book will know how to love a child and let it be who it is. They know how to trust to love."

Trust to love.

Jillian stared into space, tracing the letters on a pad of paper. They'd stayed in her head all the previous night. She had work to do, she knew, but

somehow her mind just kept circling around
Alison's phrase.

Nearly a week had gone by since Gil's bitter
words about trust. Nearly a week, and she'd
managed to survive. Work helped, anything that
would keep her busy, preferably leave her ex-
hausted and wiped out at the end. Her house,
always spotless, now positively shone with clean-
liness. The wood gleamed with beeswax, the air
held the scent of fresh pine sachets. But no matter
how much she polished and scrubbed and tidied,
she couldn't wipe away the memory of Gil
standing in her hall.

And no matter how hard she worked at her
office, she couldn't ignore the specter of him
sitting in a corner, tapping on his computer or
watching her with that lazy smile on his face.
Sometimes, she swore that she could even smell
him. Ridiculous, she lectured herself. Self-indul-
gent. She was a therapist, she knew better than
this. He was gone and she needed to forget him.

In the daylight hours she could mostly manage.
There were enough distractions to keep her from
being paralyzed with misery. It was the nights
that remained unbearable. At night, she had no
defense for the loss and emptiness that swept in.
In the darkness, between the sheets, she remembered what it had felt like to press against him.

She remembered the weight of his body on hers, the feel of him inside her. She remembered the sheer immensity of the pleasure.

And the immensity of the tenderness. In the circle of his arms, for that brief time, she'd felt safe in a way she never had before. She'd felt cared for, protected.

Loved.

Not love, she thought immediately, veering away from the thought. Sure, he'd said the words, but he couldn't possibly have meant them. If he had, he couldn't have done the things he'd done. She'd forget she'd ever heard them. She'd grown resigned to the fact that she never would.

And if she worked hard enough, she could convince herself that none of it had ever been real. So what if she still had a tendency to shake and weep without warning? So what if her emotions felt flayed? Too much had happened to her in too short a time, and she was still so worried about Robbie. They all were. She was too intelligent to confuse emotional turmoil with love.

Wasn't she?

Anyway, what was the point? It wasn't possible. Too much stood between them and she had to accept it. Maybe they had had some exquisite moments together. Not everything that felt right was meant to work out. Sometimes what seemed right was still just wrong.

And you had to figure out a way to live with it.

Her phone rang, a welcome interruption from her thoughts. "Hello?"

"Hi, Jillian? It's Scott. Logan, I mean. Your cousin."

"I think I remember you. The investigation, right?"

"Right. I've got some news."

Instantly, she was alert. "Robbie?"

"Yes. I've found him."

The relief had her smiling, for the first time in nearly a week. "Good news. Where is he?"

"Staying at a fleabag hotel in downtown Vegas. Turned out that letter he sent was a tip-off, after all."

"Have you contacted him?"

"Hell, no. You're the shrink. That's your job. I'm just the P.I., remember?"

She pulled a pad of paper toward her. "Who else knows?"

"You're the first. I'll leave it up to you to decide who else hears about it and when."

"First, I need to tell Nancy and my parents. Then we need to get everybody together right away. I'd like you to be there, too."

"Where?"

She thought a moment. "Probably here at the

clinic, don't you think? Most of us work in the area. It's central."

"Good. I can stop and see Alicia," he said, pleased. "It's, what, nine-thirty now? Let's try for ten."

"Perfect. I'll spread the word."

Lois wasn't in her office so Jillian walked down to the day care center to find Nancy supervising a group of children working with finger paints. In the week since Jillian had seen her, Nancy had grown even thinner, her smile a pale imitation of the sunbeam grin that she usually unleashed on the world.

Jillian stepped forward. "Nancy, do you have a minute?"

Nancy wiped her hands on her apron. "Of course. What's going on?"

"Good news," Jillian said. "Robbie's been found."

Nancy's face went absolutely white and she swayed.

"Sit down." Jillian guided her to a chair and pressed her head down between her knees. "Breathe."

"They've found him? Where is he?"

"I just heard from Scott. He's in Las Vegas. I didn't get the details on where—"

"I've got to go to him." Nancy straightened.

"Nancy, be smart about this. I haven't even told my parents yet. I wanted you to be first to hear. Yes, we need to go find him but we need to be cautious."

"There isn't any 'we' about it," Nancy snapped. "He's my husband and I'm going to bring him home."

It was the first time Jillian had heard her say a cross word to anyone. "We're not your enemies, Nancy. We all want him home."

Nancy gave her a despairing look. "Dawn Bruce, his probation officer, came to the house this weekend looking for him."

Jillian sucked in a breath. "What did you tell her?"

"That he was gone. What else could I say?"

"Did you tell her why?"

Nancy nodded. "I showed her the note and his resignation. She understands. She really seems to care about him but there's only so much she can do. She says she can delay as much as possible but if he's not in her office by tomorrow, he'll almost certainly have to do jail time." She stood. "So I'm going to get him, now."

Jillian shook her head. "This has to have been so hard for you. I can't imagine how worried you've been. But you can't just go rushing off. I didn't even get the hotel name from Scott, and we need to work out the right approach. If we just jump him out of the blue, there's nothing to stop him from bolting again."

Unconsciously, Nancy laid a hand on her stomach. "There's our child," she said stubbornly.

"He doesn't feel he deserves a loving wife and a family. Do you think he'll feel he deserves a child or that he's forfeited his right?" Nancy blanched and Jillian laid a hand over hers. "We can get through to him, Nancy. Everything's going to be all right. Do you trust me?"

Nancy stared at Jillian. Slowly, she nodded.

Jillian let out a breath. "Good. Call and tell Dawn we're going to have him in her office tomorrow. Don't tell her where he is, though. There's a family meeting over in the clinic conference room at ten. Come there and we'll work out what happens next." She reached out to give Nancy a hug. "We all want what's best for Robbie and you, Nancy. We're going to bring him home. Trust in that."

"All right, guys, that's what we've got so far."

Gil sat in the morning news meeting with the thirty-some-odd editors and team leaders of the *Gazette*. The long conference table was littered with coffee cups, papers, folders.

The editor in chief, Walt Pinter, rose. "Get out there and put together a paper."

The group of them headed out the door and into the cubicle farm that was the *Gazette's* news floor, already focusing on the tasks of the day ahead.

The mail cart was stopped outside Gil's office. "More of this stuff," grumbled Pat Danley, the mail clerk. "I'm getting married in three days, Reynolds. I'm going to be ticked if I throw my back out handling your mail."

"You'll survive, Danley."

"Easy for you to say." He rolled the cart forward.

Gil stepped into his office, skirting the full canvas bag that Pat had deposited next to its companions. Curious, he opened an envelope and started to read. There was a knock at his door.

"Cool, you're out of the meeting." It was Fetzer, smiling broadly. "I've got a live one, chief."

"Yeah?"

"Robbie Logan. My doc source tells me that the family's found him and they're planning to drag him back, kicking and screaming."

"Drag him back? Where is he?"

"Vegas, can you believe it?" Fetzer grinned. "If you're going to violate probation, you may as well do it right. Anyway, I need travel money."

"Travel money? For what?"

"To cover the story."

"In Vegas? I bet you want to cover the story."

"I've been on this thing for months," Fetzer protested.

And Gil thought of Jillian. "Forget it, Mark. If anyone's going to handle this one, I am."

* * *

It wasn't often that you could expect people to drop everything and show up at a midmorning meeting without notice, but she didn't come from an average family, Jillian thought as she looked around the Children's Connection conference room. She came from a special family, indeed.

She stood. "Thanks for making it on such short notice, everyone. I appreciate it and I know Nancy does. I'm sure you've all gotten the news that we've found Robbie. Or, rather, Scott has. I'll let him tell you about it."

Dark and just a little bit dangerous looking, Scott leaned back in his chair. "I called up a local guy in Vegas who owes me a couple of favors. He was able to get a lead on Robbie. I was out there yesterday morning and got a visual on him. My guy has someone on him making sure he stays put."

"Where is he?" Nancy asked, hands folded on the table before her. She appeared pale but composed. Unless you noticed that her knuckles were showing white.

"He's at the Sandstorm Motel near downtown. According to my guy, he's been doing day labor. Construction," Scott elaborated. "Working under the table. Assumed name. He's paying cash by the night at the hotel. Goes by the name of Rhett Ganz, which I assume he's shortened from Everett and Logan. Over to you." He nodded to Jillian.

Everett. The name Robbie's kidnappers had given him that he'd used most of his life. The name that she suspected deep down inside he identified with more than Robbie.

She stirred. "Thanks, Scott. So we know where he is. His probation officer told Nancy that he has until tomorrow to show up in her office. If he can do that, she might be able to avoid sending him to jail. He'll probably have to do community service on the weekends or something like that, but he won't do time. If we blow it, then he'll be facing at least some time in a cell."

She looked around at them. "Robbie's smart enough to know the kind of trouble he's courting. I guess that tells us he feels like what he's running from is worse. Our job will be to convince him that he's got a good, happy, productive life to come back to. I think, and Lois agrees with me, that our best bet is to do an intervention."

"You mean, just show up as a group?" Nancy asked.

"Exactly. I know he's not big on crowds but he knows us. We're family. Together, we can show him how much he matters, how much he means to us. It's just a matter of—"

They heard a commotion out in the hall, voices coming closer.

"You can't go in there," Jillian heard Sue object. "It's a private meeting."

"I don't give a damn," a man's voice replied, and the door to the conference room was wrenched open.

It was Gil, dark and vivid and *there* enough to take her breath away. "Sorry to interrupt," he said, not sounding sorry, at all. "This won't take long."

His eyes met hers and in simultaneous joy and despair, she knew: she was in love with him. It snapped through her like an electrical shock. She loved him. It might be her curse and it might be impossible, but it was her reality.

She just had to learn how to live with it.

He was carrying something, Jillian saw, a sack thrown over his shoulder like Santa Claus.

She searched for calm. "What are you doing here?"

"I heard you were going after Robbie."

Nancy made a noise of distress.

Jillian bristled. "How did you—"

"We've got our sources." Gil gave a humorless smile and thumped the bag to the ground. "Anyway, I figured you ought to have these."

"Who do you think you are, barging in here like this?" Terrence interrupted from behind him.

Gil turned to give him a level stare. "Gil Reynolds, editor with the *Gazette*."

"What the—" Terrence came up out of his chair.

"David," Jillian said quickly.

"Come on Dad, hear him out," David said, moving from where he'd been lounging against the wall near the door to put a hand on his father's shoulder. And aim a weather eye at Gil.

Gil gave him a nod. "I wrote an editorial this weekend about Robbie. This is the mail we've gotten in the past three days. One of the bags, anyway. I couldn't bring them all." He loosened the cord that held the canvas shut and dumped some of the letters out on the conference table.

"What was the editorial about?" Jillian asked.

Gil pulled a folded-up piece of newsprint out of his pocket and handed it to her.

And she looked down at the page.

When is enough enough? When is the debt paid? When does a man get to go on with his life? If you asked Robbie Logan, he might tell you never.

Assuming you could find him.

That's because Robbie has left Portland, tired, probably, of the unending public scrutiny and censure. When and if he returns, it will very likely be to a jail cell rather than his wife's side. You see, Robbie made the mistake of thinking that redemption was possible, that he could start again. When it comes to people who have made mistakes, though, we're not likely to cut them slack.

In the debate of nature versus nurture, there is much discussion of environment creating a stunted rose or a luxuriant weed. Genes win out, so the belief goes and so it happened with Robbie. Despite all he had gone through, Robbie ultimately did the right thing three years ago. Why, then, can't we forgive and forget? The parents and children affected by Charlie Prescott's schemes did. So did the Department of Corrections.

Why not us?

Robbie Logan was trying to redeem his life, but the wind of public outrage blew down that house of cards. Maybe it can be built again of stronger stuff. So I will say it here in this space first: you are seeing the end of the *Gazette*'s coverage of Robbie Logan.

Sometimes, enough really is enough.

The editorial was signed Gil Reynolds.

The words swam on the page before her. Stunned, Jillian looked up at him. "You wrote this?" she whispered. "Do you mean it?"

"Trust me," he said sardonically.

"All of these letters are in support of Robbie?"

"And printouts of e-mails. I thought you might be able to use them to help convince him to come home." His lips quirked. "See? Newspapers do have their uses."

She looked into his eyes, trying to gauge his mood. His face was unreadable. He'd written the editorial, brought the letters, come to find her. That had to mean something, didn't it?

Not necessarily, she realized immediately. Gil would never write an editorial just to gain her favor. If he wrote it and put his name on it, it was because he believed in the words he was setting to paper. Just as he'd have brought the letters because he thought it was the right thing to do. He'd gotten it, and that was important. But was he here only to discharge an obligation or was he here for her? Could they get past all the harsh words they'd flung at one another and find another chance?

Could she make herself trust?

Nerves warred with hope within her. She had to try, she had to. She had to make things right between them. That wasn't the most important thing, though, she reminded herself, not just then. The most important thing was bringing Robbie home.

She turned to her family. "This could be what

we need to convince Robbie if the intervention isn't enough."

"If this doesn't do it, I'm not sure what else could," Nancy said, glancing up from the letter she was reading with the first expression of hope Jillian had seen on her face in over a month. "We just need to find him in time."

"The clock's running, folks," Scott said. "He'll be off work around three. If we want to catch him, we need to roll."

"I'll put my travel agent on it," LJ said, pulling out his cell phone. "We've evolved a close, personal relationship over the past two months."

"I have a better idea," Gil interrupted. "My buddy Alan Barrett has a private jet. Assuming he's not using it, I'm sure he'd be happy to loan it for the trip. He owes me," Gil explained. "I'll just go give him a call."

Jillian watched him walk out into the hall, nerves jumping in her stomach. She had to talk with him, she had to try to set things right. He loved her, he'd told her as she'd left his condo that night. Despite everything, he'd said it.

If only he hadn't changed his mind.

"Jillian, listen to this," Nancy said excitedly.

"Our son Chad has been at the Children's Connection day care center for a year. I've never seen a better-run facility. Mr. and Mrs. Logan are unfailingly cheerful, kind and patient. By all means, hire Robbie back."

"That's great, Nancy." Jillian glanced back over to Gil, in the hall. She took a deep breath. She had to remain calm, but it was hard to do when she felt her entire life was hanging in the balance. Suddenly, she noticed David watching her as he leaned against the wall, a little half smile on his face. As she looked at him, he gave her a wink.

"Alan says the jet's out at the executive airport," Gil announced, walking back in. "Assuming you're ready to go, you could be there this afternoon."

"We," a voice said. Jillian looked over to see David giving a genial smile. "We could be there."

"We?" Gil echoed. "I kind of figured this was a family show."

"Not at all. The letters are a key part of the effort. I think you need to go along to vouch for the bag. Besides—" he straightened to throw an affable arm around Gil's shoulders "—it'll give us a chance to get to know you. I'm David Logan, by the way. Jillian's twin brother."

Chapter Sixteen

It seemed patently unfair to Jillian that all she wanted to do was get five minutes alone with Gil and suddenly that was the last thing that was possible. Robbie, she reminded herself as the entire Logan clan, plus miscellaneous spouses and Gil, carpooled out to the airport. Robbie was the important one here, especially with Nancy looking as though she was holding on with her last bit of nerve. They needed to get Robbie home. Everything else could wait, however little Jillian might want it to.

So it was that she found herself standing with the rest in the hangar at Hillsboro Airport, watching the mechanics and pilots ready Alan Barrett's jet to tow out. Jillian walked about restlessly, shivering in the shade of the building.

The she saw Gil standing alone out on the tarmac, watching a green-and-yellow Cessna that had just started up. Her mother had shepherded Nancy off; everyone else was involved in other conversations. Jillian took a deep breath and walked out into sunlight.

"Gil?"

He turned to her. "Hey."

"Hi." She couldn't read his expression behind his sunglasses.

"Ready to go?"

"As ready as I can be," she said. "There's a lot up in the air."

"Give it a few minutes and we will be, too."

They were already, she thought, searching for a way to start. She was a therapist; emotions were her stock-in-trade. She knew what she wanted to tell him. Why, then, was she standing here staring at him, tongue-tied?

Begin at the beginning.

Instead, she cleared her throat. "I just wanted to say thank you. For the editorial, for bringing the letters, for coming here. Thank you for everything you've done."

He seemed disappointed, somehow. "I went

back and looked at the articles we'd done on Robbie. They didn't tell the whole story. The editorial finished it."

"It pretty much said it all."

He nodded. "All I had to say."

All? she wondered.

Across the apron, the Cessna began to move, propeller whirling.

Begin at the beginning, Jillian told herself, rubbing her arms. "About the other night," she began.

He turned to look at her then. "Yeah?"

"You said some things."

"We both said a lot of things."

"You were right about some of them. A lot of them." She watched the Cessna roll toward the runway. "I don't let a lot of people in. I never have. When you learn things as a kid, it's hard to change those habits."

Gil put his hands in his pockets. "Given what you learned as a kid, I think it's a damned miracle that you've become who you are."

"I could be better," she said.

"We all could be. And sometimes we make one another better. Isn't that part of what being with people is all about? I'm a better person because of you. I've learned things."

"What I said about your work at the paper was

wrong. I understand why you had to run the story about Robbie. That doesn't mean I liked it but I understand why you did it. I was wrong to say otherwise. I'm sorry."

"Don't be. You made me think. I've always told myself I did my job for the community but I've never let myself become a part of it. You taught me how."

He pushed up his glasses and looked at her. Suddenly, it was as though nobody else was there, just the two of them. And it was like it always was with him, the immediate connection, as though they were looking inside each other. He was a man of honor and bravery and she loved him. She'd tried to fight it, tried to deny it but there was no point. Her heart was his. He was the man she loved and he had given them a chance, a chance for happiness.

She just had to find the courage to grasp at it. "When I talked with you the other night, before we…"

"Made love?" he supplied gently when she colored.

She nodded. "I had no idea when I got to your house how I was ever going to tell you. It seemed too enormous. I was absolutely tied in knots over it. But you made it easy."

"I care about you, Jillian. It wasn't hard to listen."

I care about you. What had happened to "I love you"? she wondered. Had he changed his mind?

Out on the runway, the Cessna was taxiing, gathering speed. She had to take the risk, Jillian realized. She had to trust. Taking a deep breath, she made herself meet his eyes. "I missed you this week. I thought about you all the time."

"Not nearly as much as I thought about you," he said.

She wanted to look away but she made herself hold his gaze. She swallowed. "I don't have a lot of practice opening up but I want to learn. I want to be with you, Gil. I want to see if we can make this work."

"You mean that?"

With a roar, the Cessna lifted into the air.

And suddenly, miraculously, it was easy. "I love you, Gil. I realized it the minute you walked in today, before you ever said a word. I want you in my life. I don't know what shape that will take, I don't care. I just need you there. I love you," she repeated.

She'd barely gotten the words out before he wrapped his arms around her. "Say it again," he demanded.

"I love you."

He fused his mouth to hers and the joy bubbled up inside her. "God, Jillian, you have no idea what this week was like. I thought I'd lost you forever."

"Not a chance," she said, smiling into his eyes. "You got under my skin too far to ever get you out."

"I love you," he said. "I thought I was just going to go nuts when you walked out last week. We're going to make this work, I don't care what it takes."

"Of course we will," she said. "Because it's right."

Gil parked the rental van down the street from the Sandstorm Motel, before a stucco building painted with murals. The motel was cramped and seedy and old, packed into a small lot off to one side of downtown. The plastic sign was missing a chunk at the bottom so that the fluorescent tubes showed through. Cracked and peeling paint covered the trim.

The van was packed with Logan siblings, parents and cousins. They'd rented three at the airport, enough to fit them all. He didn't really care about any of them, though, except Jillian, in the seat beside him.

Beside him. Gil squeezed her hand. Half of him was incredulous with joy. Even the three-hour flight hadn't given him time to get used to it. He couldn't quite believe that everything was suddenly so right. He was afraid that he would blink and she would change her mind.

So much depended on Robbie, though, he thought, feeling the tension gather in his shoulders. If things didn't work with Robbie, would she still feel the same or would she come to blame him when her brother was in jail?

And would her family?

Terrence Logan hadn't looked all that thrilled when he'd realized that Gil and his daughter were together. He'd warmed over the course of the flight enough to at least stop frowning at Gil. It would get easier over time. If Gil had anything to say about it, Terrence would have plenty of time to get used to it.

If only they could bring Robbie home.

"This is him," Scott said suddenly, as a faded green pickup that had clearly seen better days made a left turn into the parking lot of the motel and disappeared into the back. "Okay. We'll let him go in and then in about fifteen minutes go up."

It was more like thirty by the time they got grouped together beside the hotel.

Scott nodded to Jillian. "You're the shrink. What do we do?" he asked softly.

Jillian turned to Nancy. "You and I should go up to the door, first. Then we play it by ear. Dad, maybe you and Mom could step in. The idea is to make it clear that we need him home, that we love him."

In twos and threes, they walked down to Robbie's unit and gathered out in the parking lot before the door. Jillian nodded to Nancy. Swallowing, Nancy stepped forward and knocked on the door.

"Yeah?" a voice called.

"Robbie?" She licked her lips. "Are you in there?"

She waited but there was no response. "Robbie?" she said again.

"Nancy?" With a rattle of the chain, the door whipped open and he stood there. "What are you doing here?"

Jillian bit back a gasp at his appearance. Never stocky, he'd lost so much weight in the time he'd been gone she hardly recognized him. Scott had been right about the construction work—he was so tan he looked almost swarthy. His arms were ropy with muscle.

He stared at Nancy. "Why are you here?"

"Because I miss you," she said softly.

"You shouldn't have come," he said.

"I couldn't stay away. You're my husband, Robbie." Her eyes were pleading. "I love you."

"We're all here because we love you," Jillian said, stepping forward. "And we want to bring you home."

He looked beyond, then, seeing the cluster of them move into view. A glint of panic flickered in his eyes. "It's no good," he said.

"Let us in, Robbie," Jillian said gently.

He turned his back on them, stepping into the room. "Portland's not my home anymore."

"And this is?" Jillian looked around the room

where he had lived for almost two months and shook her head. Unidentifiable stains marked the muddy beige carpet. The walls were a dispirited tan. A synthetic coverlet in avocado-green and orange covered the bed. The plastic of the television casing was cracked.

"Would you really rather stay here than go home?" Nancy asked.

"Nobody wants me in Portland."

Terrence stepped into the room after them. "You're on probation, son. You've got to go back."

"Dawn doesn't even know I'm gone," he said with a hint of bravado.

"She knows," Nancy said. "If you're in her office tomorrow, everything will be okay. If not, they'll put a warrant out for your arrest." Her eyes were full of misery. "They'll put you in jail, Robbie."

"So what." An edge entered his voice. "Do you think it's any worse than all the stories and the sneers? Walking into a store and hearing people saying things behind my back? Everyone hates me."

"They don't." Gil walked into the room with his bag. He didn't say anything more, just emptied it out on the bed until the pile of envelopes threatened to spill off the edge.

"What are those?" Robbie asked, staring.

"Letters to the editor of the *Portland Gazette,*" Gil said. He picked one up and yanked out the letter inside. "'I want to say I think Robbie Logan's gotten a raw deal from the *Gazette*. He's a good man who deserves better.' Phil Burns, Lake Oswego." He tossed it down.

"'It's not what people did in the past, it's who they are now,'" Jillian read from another. "'People can grow and change. That's what redemption is all about. Bring Robbie Logan home.' Tanya Simms, Tigard."

"'Bravo on your editorial on redemption,'" Nancy read with a shaking voice. "'Don't we have better things to do than hound Robbie Logan? Let the man go on with his life.' Tom Mahoney, Portland."

Robbie snatched up one of the envelopes and pulled out the letter inside. Silently, he read it and his hands began to shake.

"Read it," Jillian said.

"'It's about time we called the dogs off. Robbie Logan did the right thing and now we need to do the right thing. Come home, Robbie.'" His voice was barely audible. "'We're sorry.' Ron Hitchens, Oregon City."

"They really want me back?" he asked in wonder.

"What have we been telling you?" Jillian asked.

Nancy walked up to him and he put his arms around her and buried his face in her neck. "We love you, Robbie, all of us. Not just me but your family, the people at the clinic, all the people whose lives you've touched. Can't you understand that?"

"Sometimes it's hard to believe," he said. "Sometimes it's hard to really trust."

Jillian's gaze flicked to Gil's.

"Maybe you'll trust that you're going to be the best father in the world," Nancy told him, putting Robbie's hand on her stomach.

He stiffened and stared at her. "The best father?"

"The best father," she said lightly, but she watched him closely and her voice was filled with strain.

An incredulous grin spread across his face. "I'm going to be a dad?"

"In about seven months."

He wrapped his arms around her and raised her off her feet.

And then it was bedlam, with everyone crowding around, hugging him and shaking his hand. Finally, Robbie held Nancy's hands in his and smiled down at her. "Well, I don't know about the rest of you but I need to get back to Portland. If I'm going to be a dad, I've got to get my life in gear."

And smiling through her tears, she wrapped her arms around his neck.

"Let's get you out of here, son," said Terrence. "It's time to go home."

Gil and Jillian stepped outside and into the heat of the Las Vegas afternoon. Back in the room, the rest of the family was helping Robbie pack up what few belongings he had.

"You did it," Gil said.

She squeezed his hand. "You did it. All the talk in the world would never have been enough. It was the letters that convinced him. We owe you."

"You owe me?" he repeated. "Then I guess I'd better collect on that." He ran his fingertips down her bare arm, and she shivered.

"I don't know, what do you want?"

He swung her around to face him. "Oh, to get you naked and have my way with you for about two weeks straight."

Her eyes darkened. "I'm sure that could be arranged."

"Or to hear you say 'I love you' to me every day for the next couple of dozen years."

"I can definitely do that."

Laughing, Gil swung her around. And suddenly he saw it, the white stucco building with the murals, where they'd parked. Murals of brides and grooms, walking among trees. A Vegas wedding chapel, he realized.

A Vegas wedding chapel.

And that quickly, he knew what he really wanted.

"What I really want is to marry you," he said.

Her eyes flew open. "What?"

He pressed his lips to hers. "Marry me, Jillian.

You're all that I've ever wanted." He looked down at her.

Her mouth moved but no words escaped.

Behind them, the Logan clan filtered out of the motel parking lot.

"What's going on here?" David asked.

"Do you mind giving us some privacy?" Gil said without looking away. "I'm proposing."

"I don't know, dude, she doesn't seem to be answering," Scott said as he came up behind David. "Maybe you should ask her again. Maybe she didn't hear."

"Maybe she's playing hard to get," LJ suggested. "They do that, sometimes," he said, glancing at Eden, who wore his ring on her finger.

"Yes," Jillian burst out, throwing her arms around Gil. "Oh, yes, yes, yes. And I hate you all," she added, glowering at Eric and David and LJ.

"What did we do?" Eric protested. "We were just being supportive."

"You turned my proposal into a stand-up comedy routine."

"Turned what into a stand-up comedy routine?" Leslie said, coming up behind them. "What have you boys done now?"

"Oh, hell," David said, "now we're in trouble."

"Watch your mouth, young man."

"We're never going to hear the end of this," Eric said.

"I'm guessing you're right," LJ confirmed, watching his father approach uneasily.

"I'll do it again if I can get a little bit of quiet," Gil said, and took Jillian's hands. This time, he went down on one knee before her. "Jillian Logan, I know few things for certain but one of them is that I absolutely, totally and completely love you. You're all I want and all I need. I'll spend the rest of my life making you happy. Will you marry me?"

She took his face in her hands and kissed him. "I will."

White satin. Ribbons and lace. The chapel echoed with the liquid tones of water falling into the stone fountain at the end. Ivy trailed around the white pillars at the altar. Jasmine from the bouquets scented the air. And everywhere faces glowed with that luminous joy unique to weddings.

Jillian waited at the back of the aisle, where she'd stood so many times before. Family filled the white wrought iron chairs. And at the front, bouncing lightly in anticipation, stood the bridegroom.

Gil.

She started down the aisle, a clutch of jasmine in her hands, her fingertips on the arm of her father. For once, she wasn't a bridesmaid; this time, she was the bride.

When they reached the front and Terrence kissed her cheek, she felt the tears threaten. Then he placed her hands in Gil's and she thought her heart was just going to explode with joy.

Love. Honor. Till death do us part. The same words, said so many times, were new as she spoke them. She felt Gil slide the ring onto her finger.

And as she looked at him she saw her future in his eyes.

"I love you," she said.

And when they kissed, she knew it was forever.

* * * * *

THE ROYAL HOUSE OF NIROLI
Always passionate, always proud.

The richest royal family in the world—united by blood and passion, torn apart by deceit and desire.

Nestled in the azure blue of the Mediterranean Sea, the majestic island of Niroli has prospered for centuries. The Fierezza men have worn the crown with passion and pride since ancient times. But now, as the king's health declines and his two sons have been tragically killed, the crown is in jeopardy.

The clock is ticking—a new heir must be found before the king is forced to abdicate. By royal decree the internationally scattered members of the Fierezza family are summoned to claim their destiny. But any person who takes the throne must do so according to The Rules of the Royal House of Niroli. Soon secrets and rivalries emerge as the descendents of this ancient royal line vie for position and power. Only a true Fierezza can become ruler—a person dedicated to their country, their people…and their eternal love!

Each month, starting in July 2007,
Harlequin Presents is delighted to bring you
an exciting installment from
THE ROYAL HOUSE OF NIROLI,
in which you can follow the epic search
for the true Nirolian king.
Eight heirs, eight romances, eight fantastic stories!

Here's your chance to enjoy a sneak preview of the first book delivered to you by royal decree….

FIVE minutes later she was standing immobile in front of the study's window, her original purpose of coming in forgotten, as she stared in shocked horror at the envelope she was holding. Waves of heat followed by icy chill surged through her body. She could hardly see the address now through her blurred vision, but the crest on its left-hand front corner stood out, its *royal* crest, followed by the address: *HRH Prince Marco of Niroli*....

She didn't hear Marco's key in the apartment door, she didn't even hear him calling out her name. Her shock was so great that nothing could penetrate it. It encased her in a kind of bubble, which only concentrated the torment of what she was suffering and branded it on her brain so that it could never be forgotten. It was only finally pierced by the sudden opening of the study door as Marco walked in.

"Welcome home, *Your Highness.* I suppose I ought to curtsy." She waited, praying that he would laugh and tell her that she had got it all wrong, that the envelope she was holding, addressing him as Prince Marco of Niroli, was some silly mistake. But like a tiny candle flame shivering vulnerably in the dark, her hope trembled fearfully. And then the look in Marco's eyes extinguished it as cruelly as a hand placed callously over a dying person's face to stem their last breath.

"Give that to me," he demanded, taking the envelope from her.

"It's too late, Marco," Emily told him brokenly. "I know the truth now…" She dug her teeth in her lower lip to try to force back her own pain.

"You had no right to go through my desk," Marco shot back at her furiously, full of loathing at being caught off guard and forced into a position in which he was in the wrong, making him determined to find something he could accuse Emily of. "I trusted you…."

Emily could hardly believe what she was

hearing. "No, you didn't trust me, Marco, and you didn't trust me because you knew that I couldn't trust you. And you knew that because you're a liar; and liars don't trust people because they know that they themselves cannot be trusted." She not only felt sick, she also felt as though she could hardly breathe. "You are Prince Marco of Niroli... How could you not tell me who you are and still live with me as intimately as we have lived together?" she demanded brokenly.

"Stop being so ridiculously dramatic," Marco demanded fiercely. "You are making too much of the situation."

"*Too much?*" Emily almost screamed the words at him. "When were you going to tell me, Marco? Perhaps you just planned to walk away without telling me anything? After all, what do my feelings matter to you?"

"Of course they matter." Marco stopped her sharply. "And it was in part to protect them, and you, that I decided not to inform you when my grandfather first announced that he intended to step down from the throne and hand it over to me."

"To protect me?" Emily nearly choked on her fury. "Hand on the throne? No wonder you told me when you first took me to bed that all you wanted was sex. You *knew* that was the only kind of relationship there could ever be between us! You *knew*

that one day you would be Niroli's king. No doubt
you are expected to marry a princess. Is she picked
out for you already, your *royal* bride?"

* * * * *

Look for
THE FUTURE KING'S PREGNANT MISTRESS
by Penny Jordan in July 2007,
from Harlequin Presents,
available wherever books are sold.

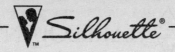

SPECIAL EDITION™

Emotional, compelling stories that capture the intensity of living, loving and creating a family in today's world.

Modern, passionate reads that are powerful and provocative.

nocturne

Dramatic and sensual tales of paranormal romance.

Romances that are sparked by danger and fueled by passion.

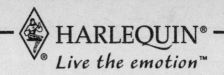

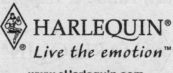

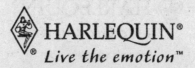

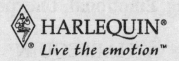

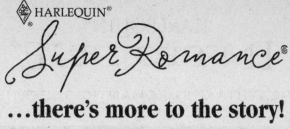
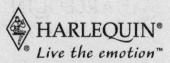

Harlequin® Historical
Historical Romantic Adventure!

Imagine a time of chivalrous knights and unconventional ladies, roguish rakes and impetuous heiresses, rugged cowboys and spirited frontierswomen—— these rich and vivid tales will capture your imagination!

Harlequin Historical . . . they're too good to miss!

HHDIR06